I0772963

Jane Daly

Heart of a Hero

Jane Daly

Chapter 1

Simone cranked up the volume on the car stereo and raised her voice to belt out the chorus to Toby Mac's Promised Land. Even the traffic backed up on the Marion Bridge heading west toward Main, Oregon, couldn't dampen her relief at leaving her parents' house.

Sunday lunches at the folk's used to be something to look forward to, but lately the continual drama got on Simone's last nerve. Simone loved her family, but at times the safety net of her parents nearby felt more like a snare.

Her seven-year-old Honda surged forward when the traffic finally thinned out. Simone passed a white pickup going exactly the speed limit. No one did the speed limit on this stretch of highway. Shaking her head, she pressed harder on the accelerator, surprised when a motorcycle sped past her.

A few miles later, Simone caught up to the motorcycle. It weaved from side to side in the lane, then to her horror, sped off the highway and onto a grassy berm on the right side of the road. A plume of dust rose from the field.

Simone yanked the steering wheel to the right and slammed on the brakes, her car coming to rest with a shuddering stop. She jammed a finger on the emergency flashers, jumped out of the car, and sprinted to where the motorcycle lay on its side.

A man lay face down in the weeds. His half-helmet rolled a few feet away. Simone laid two fingers on the man's neck, searching for a pulse. Nothing. Fearful of a neck or spine injury, she waited only a moment before grabbing his arm and pulling him onto his back.

The guy's lips were blue and his face devoid of color. She started chest compressions, willing his heart to resume its job of giving life.

~

Gabriel Harrison set the cruise control of his pickup at exactly fifty-five. He couldn't afford another speeding ticket. He grimaced, thinking about his latest insurance bill.

An orange Honda buzzed past him, followed by a motorcycle. For a brief moment, he allowed himself a bit of self-pity over selling his beloved Harley. He understood why his fireman buddies called hogs 'organ donors.'

As a first responder, Gabriel had seen his share of deadly motorcycle collisions. Dying on the hard pavement was a poor substitute for the wind on his face and the feeling of total freedom.

The clock on his dash showed he'd arrive at his parents' house in Main in time for a shower before dinner. They'd promised him a full-on roast beef dinner to celebrate his return, temporary though it was.

One month and he'd be back on the job in Portland. This thirty-day leave of absence to help his parents would give him the opportunity to train for the most grueling personal challenge ever. Since the events of September 11, thousands of firefighters around the country reenacted the stairs climbed by the first responders in the Twin Towers.

Last year, Gabe had intended to sign up, but his girlfriend at the time made plans for them to take a cruise. Now that Tiffany was no longer in the picture, there'd be no distractions to keep him from crossing this event off his bucket list.

From a distance, Gabe saw flashing emergency lights from a car stopped on the side of the road. As he got closer, he recognized the unique orange color of the Honda that passed him on Highway 22. He pulled to a stop a few feet behind the vehicle, stepped out of his truck, and approached the car. Empty.

"Help! Over here!" The female voice called from somewhere in the grassy field.

Gabe sprinted through the weeds and found a dark-skinned woman doing CPR on a thirty-something-looking man. His gaze took in the crumpled motorcycle and the upside-down helmet.

"Here, take my phone and call 9-1-1." Gabe shouldered the woman out of the way while handing her his phone. He pressed the man's chest, then leaned down to listen for the sound of breath.

"I left my phone in the car," the woman said as she fumbled with Gabe's phone.

Gabe bit back a sarcastic response and pressed again on the man's chest. He continued CPR until the man took a gasping inhale.

He heard the girl telling the 9-1-1 operator where they were and the situation.

"Good job, buddy," Gabe said. He tilted the man's head back enough for him to breathe more easily. He watched with satisfaction as color returned to the guy's lips.

~

Simone stayed on the phone with the operator until the sound of approaching sirens filled the air. She disconnected and leaned over to hand the phone to the stranger. She watched as he gently lifted each of the guy's eyelids to check his pupils, ignoring her outstretched hand.

He rubbed his hands down each of the downed cyclist's legs before gently palpitating his abdomen. While half of her brain registered shock at the accident, the other half couldn't help noticing how his muscles flexed under the thin tee shirt stretched over his large frame.

His calf muscles bunched as he pushed himself to his feet. Simone took only a moment to admire his shorts-clad legs before thrusting the phone toward him.

"Thanks," he said.

Before Simone could respond, the whine of sirens rose to a crescendo when two firetrucks and an ambulance pulled over, followed by an Oregon State Trooper.

Soon the grassy field was filled with male first responders. They approached the handsome stranger, their questions rapid-firing at him.

"What happened?"

"How long was he without air?"

"Any broken bones?"

"Did you see the accident?"

Simone found herself pushed out of the way of the

paramedics who carried a backboard and IV supplies.

"Ma'am, you'll have to step out of the way."

"But—"

The paramedic didn't wait for her to finish.

Simone watched as the muscular stranger was congratulated by the men who now surrounded him. She could barely make out the words, but it sounded like he was taking full credit for saving the guy's life.

The downed cyclist was loaded into the ambulance and its siren wound up again and started off down the road.

Simone sucked in a breath and blew it out through pursed lips. She tried making eye contact with the presumed life-saver, but he was too busy shaking hands and grinning like an idiot.

Fine. Let him get the glory. Simone was sure there was a verse in the Bible somewhere about humility. She couldn't bring it to mind at that moment.

Still fuming, Simone hopped in her car and headed toward Main. She had barely enough time to get to town for the weekly meeting with her two best friends. Wait until Lizzy and Mariah heard about the glory hog.

Chapter 2

By the time he'd given his statement to the State Trooper, the crowd of first responders had thinned. Gabe glanced around, hoping to see the woman who had arrived on the scene of the accident before him. Gone.

Guilt stabbed his chest over taking credit for saving the cyclist's life. Had the woman thought to grab her cell phone when she'd exited her vehicle, she'd be the one taking all the congratulations.

Sheesh. Who didn't carry their phone like an extra appendage? Still, Gabe had noticed her hazel eyes, wide with fear. At least she'd had the sense to begin CPR. But who was she? Her exotic looks indicated some kind of mixed heritage. Black hair, hazel eyes, and dark skin.

In a town the size of Main, Oregon, he was bound to run into her somewhere.

He hoped.

Now to get to his parents' house and explain why he was late for his homecoming dinner.

"Gabriel, honey, I'm glad you're here."

Gabe's mom pulled him into a fierce hug. When she stepped back, Gabe noticed new lines around her mouth and dark circles under her eyes.

"Let him go, Deb," Dad said, grabbing his hand and pulling him in for his own hug.

Gabe allowed himself to rest in his parents' enjoyment before giving himself some distance.

"Where's Grace?"

"Your sister is resting." Mom lowered her voice. "This has been difficult for all of us. I'm glad you're here to help."

A moment later, two little girls burst into the house and launched themselves at Gabe's legs.

"Uncle Gabe!" they said in unison.

"Shh, girls, your mom is sleeping," Mom admonished. "Let's go into the kitchen."

The two girls planted themselves on Gabe's feet, forcing him to shuffle flat-footed, giggling as he dragged them toward the kitchen.

Gabe's stomach growled as the smell of roasted meat, potatoes, and carrots permeated the house.

"Come sit and tell us why you're late," Mom said.

Gabe's dad picked up one of his nieces and planted her on a booster seat at the table. With a twinkle in his eye, he said, "Which one are you? Mercy?"

Gabe's niece giggled. "No, silly. I'm Hope."

"Are you sure?" Dad asked.

"I'm Mercy," the girl's twin said.

"John, stop teasing the girls and get them up to the table," Mom said with a frown.

Gabe didn't blame his dad. He'd never been able to tell his sister's twins apart.

While he ate the best pot roast ever, Gabe told his parents about the motorcycle accident, downplaying his role in saving the guy's life. He glossed over the woman who'd arrived at the scene first.

"You're a hero, Son."

Gabe basked in his dad's approval. Dad was his hero. He always made the right choices, even if it meant being taken advantage of. Gabe envied his dad's unwavering faith, wishing he still carried the zeal for God he'd had in his younger years.

He was here now, to help his dad with the fall seed harvest. Mom had her hands full watching Mercy and Hope while his sister struggled in the final month of her difficult pregnancy. Her husband, Demarcus, hoped to fly home from his deployment overseas in time for the baby's birth.

Gabe planned to be gone before then. Back to Portland. Or maybe someplace different. He still waited for a response from the job inquiry he'd sent to the fire department in South Carolina. Anyplace he wouldn't run into Tiffany.

~

Simone strode into Cookie's Café, still irked by the glory hog at the motorcycle accident. She spotted her friends at a table outside. Why couldn't they sit inside where the air conditioner kept the heat where it belonged? The overhead fans on the patio tried to cool the area. And failed.

Mariah looked up and caught Simone's eye. "Come sit by me. I have exciting news." She swept her gaze over Simone's face. "What happened to you?"

Simone dropped onto a chair with a sigh. "Your news first."

Mariah shook her head. "Nope. You look like something my future stepson dragged in from the mud."

"Thank you, Mariah. Always so blunt." Simone

smiled despite herself. "You would not believe the day I've had."

"Spill it, girlfriend," Lizzy said, scrunching her forehead.

Simone started her story with the motorcycle that buzzed past her on Highway 22 and ended with being shoved out of the way by one of the first responders.

"All that one guy did was take over so I could call 9-1-1."

"Do you know who he was?" Mariah asked.

"No, but what a glory hog." Simone's mouth turned down in disgust.

"Typical male," Mariah commented. "Except for mine and Lizzy's," she added with a smirk.

Simone rested her hands on the table. "What's this exciting news?"

Mariah practically bounced in her seat. "Ethan and I have finally set a date."

"Great!" Simone gave the expected response, but her heart was anything but enthusiastic. Since her breakup with Adam, it felt like everyone else was living their happily ever after dream while she was stuck in a dead-end job in a dead-end town.

As Mariah gushed about a Winter wedding, Simone's thoughts returned to the conversation she'd had with her parents and her little sister over lunch. Their plans seemed to change every other month. Two years ago, they were going to move to Idaho to help Simone's older sister, Eva, with her triplets. Simone was staying behind so Olivia could finish high school. Then Covid hit, and her parents stayed put.

Now they were talking about moving to California. Since Olivia's diagnosis, they thought a less rainy climate might do her little sister good. Simone hoped they'd actually go this time. Then she wouldn't feel guilty about wanting to leave too.

Her parents' apron strings were like a long leash. They yanked Simone's chain enough – their unconscious tether a sharp reminder she remained stuck.

With a sigh, Simone turned her attention back to Mariah's plans.

"I hope you'll both be bridesmaids."

"As long as you don't choose some hideous color for our dresses," Lizzy said.

Mariah narrowed her eyes. "Like what?"

"Like salmon or rust," Lizzy responded. "Remember, I have fair skin and need a color to complement me. Simone has darker skin and needs a dress to look great on her."

"Spoken like a true interior designer," Simone said, reaching across the table to smack her friend's shoulder.

Lizzy grinned. "Only two more months and I'll be finished with school." She placed a hand on her growing baby bump. "Let's hope this one waits until I'm done to be born."

"I'm not sure you have a choice about that."

"Speaking of, when's your due date again?" Mariah asked, pulling out her cell phone.

"December thirty-first," Lizzy answered. "Please don't tell me that's your wedding date."

Mariah laughed. "Nope. It's December twelfth. My mom promised to outdo herself with Christmas decorations at the vineyard. We'll have the wedding there, of course."

"Of course," Lizzy and Simone answered simultaneously.

Mariah's parents owned a vineyard at the top of a mountain with a hundred and eighty-degree view of the valley. Mariah's wedding would be the social event of the season. If Main had a season, that is.

Main hadn't grown much since Simone moved here at the start of middle school. Main's population included a smattering of people of different ethnic backgrounds, and the middle school had a total of three Black kids. She and Lizzy had immediately bonded, Simone as the new girl and Lizzy as the social outcast.

With a White mother and Black father, Simone fit into neither camp. She and Lizzy formed a tight twosome that lasted into their adulthood.

Mariah had recently been admitted to their minuscule clique. Since middle school, Mariah and her friends bullied Simone and Lizzy. They'd had lots of ammunition when Simone returned from Bible Camp at her grandmother's church in Georgia with a zeal for Jesus she didn't hesitate to share.

Everything changed when Mariah's fiancé broke up with her when she tried to trap him into marriage by trying to get pregnant. Mariah turned to the church for help and ended up a changed person. Lizzy had embraced Mariah's change with open arms, but Simone had been slower to accept Mariah 2.0.

A year later, Simone was glad she did. Mariah turned out to be a good listener and quick to give advice, even when it hurt. After Simone's breakup with Adam, Mariah stepped in with a comforting shoulder and lots of admonition that Simone was better off without him.

"Look at me," Mariah had exclaimed. "My guy took off and now Ethan is my rock. God has someone for you. You'll see."

Mariah was engaged to Main Community Church's youth pastor. His wife had been killed by a drunk driver, leaving him a single dad, trying to raise a five-year-old boy.

A sliver of envy snaked up Simone's back. Her long-time bestie, Lizzy was married to Roman who was the perfect stepdad to Lizzy's daughter, Abigail. Mariah was engaged to a handsome youth pastor.

Meanwhile, Simone was, well, single and destined to stay that way for a long time.

Chapter 3

Gabe groaned as the bright morning sun pierced through the thin blinds of his childhood bedroom. He swung his arm over to block the light and took a deep breath, inhaling the familiar scent of coffee brewing in the kitchen below. Dad must have been up for hours, tending to their farm.

He ran his hand through his messy hair and rubbed his unshaven face. The stubble had to go. But coffee first, then shave.

Nothing had changed in his bedroom since he left for college. His sports trophies still adorned the shelves and his mother had even framed his admission letter from Portland State University, where he had received a full-ride baseball scholarship.

All good memories. Work hard, play hard, and celebrate hard. Somewhere along the way, he'd lost a part of himself.

Raised in a strict Christian household, Gabe had strayed from faith and mistakes with Tiffany were worldly made. Facing his parents' disappointment would be unbearable.

He'd justified avoiding the parents for a million reasons.

"I have to work over Christmas."

"They scheduled me over Thanksgiving."

"I'm the only guy without a wife and kids. I volunteered to work over Easter."

But Gabe's sister's tearful request gutted him. Grace knew how to tear down his defenses with one simple request.

"Please come help, Gabe. Mom is having to wrangle Hope and Mercy while I'm on bed rest. She can't help Dad, and neither can I. Please, Gabey." Grace's tears did him in.

Reluctantly, Gabe agreed to take four weeks off work and return to the small town where it all began for him. Four weeks to keep his secrets hidden from his family. Four weeks before he could escape back to the anonymity of the city, where no one knew about the mess he had made of his life.

Four hours later, Dad had walked Gabe around the seed farm. Gabe had a good idea of what he'd be doing for the next month. Fatigued thinking about it, Gabe headed to the gym. His buddy, Carson owned one of Main's gyms, and he'd promised to find Gabe a personal trainer. Someone who'd prepare him for the stair climb in September.

Carson greeted Gabe with the back-slapping and friendly bro hug expected among old friends.

"Glad to see you're back home," Carson said. "Have a seat." Carson pointed to a plastic chair in front of a messy desk. "Excuse the mess. My admin quit and I haven't been able to replace her yet."

"No problem," Gabe responded, glancing the chaos.

Carson leaned back in his chair and laced his hands

behind his head. "Heard you had a little excitement yesterday."

Gabe frowned. "What did you hear?"

"Oh, come on, man. You know small towns. You can't burp without someone knowing. You saved a guy's life.

Gabe's shoulders slumped. Small-town gossip. One reason he'd been glad to see Main in his rearview mirror. Every movement, every decision, was viewed by everyone within a three-mile radius.

"I guess," Gabe responded.

"No, dude. That was epic."

Let it go, *dude*. Gabe leaned forward and rested his hands on his thighs. "Look, man, I do stuff like that every day."

Carson's laugh grated on Gabe's last nerve.

Carson's chair fell and thumped onto the floor. "Don't be surprised if the paparazzi show up to get a picture of our hometown hero."

Gabe frowned as Carson continued. "Anyway, tell me about this stair climb thing."

"It's intense," Gabe said. "Every year in September, there's a reenactment of the stairs the first responders had to climb on 9/11. We wear all our gear and do it in memory of the men and women who died trying to save the people trapped."

Carson stared at him for a moment. "I have the perfect trainer for you. She'll make sure you're able to take on the challenge."

"Sounds good. When do I meet her?"

Carson pulled his laptop closer. "She's scheduled all day. I'll look for her and bring her into the office for a quick meet-and-greet."

Gabe leaned back. He'd never worked with a female personal trainer before. When he played baseball, the trainers were guys who'd either been injured playing and could no longer compete, or men working on their PT degree at the University. He trusted Carson, but could a woman really prepare him for the 9/11 stair challenge? Doubtful.

His friend's gym might have been a mistake. In small town Main, how could there possibly be a competent personal trainer? No one with any kind of experience would find a decent career here. He'd make nice for one session and then do some research to find someone in Salem.

~

Simone laid her hand on her client's shoulder. "Good job, Art. You're coming along great."

Art smiled at her from his seat on the recumbent bike. "Thank you, Simone. I hope to be back on the golf course soon."

Simone smiled. "You will. Keep working that knee. Are you doing the exercises I gave you?"

Art nodded. "My wife nags me all day about it. After forty-nine years you'd think I'd be used to it by now." He chuckled, taking the ire out of his words.

Simone squeezed his shoulder before letting her hand drop. "You better listen to her. She probably wants you back on the golf course to get out of her hair."

"You've got that right."

"Give me ten more minutes on the bike, then we'll do some cool-down stretches before you go home, okay?"

Art gave her a mock salute and continued to pedal.

Simone spied her boss, Carson, motioning her to come to his office.

"I'll be back in a minute, Art."

She navigated through the machines, catching up with Carson outside the administrative office. "What's up?"

"I have a new client for you. Come on in and I'll introduce you. Although, you might know him. He went to high school here. What year did you graduate?"

"2014."

Carson's eyes shifted left, doing mental calculations. He shrugged. "Well, anyway, you may know him."

Simone tossed Art a glance. "Can it wait a minute? I'm finishing up with Art Johnson." She glanced at her watch. "Actually, he'll be done in eight minutes and then we have cool down."

Carson bounced on his toes. "This won't take long. A quick intro and I'll let you go. You can connect with him after you're done with Art."

"I guess." Who was Carson connecting her with now? He sloughed off clients he didn't want. Elderly people recovering from hip or knee replacement surgery, like Art. Women wanting quick weight loss for a wedding dress. Simone's feet dragged as she followed Carson into his office.

The sight of someone with a youthful head of hair pleasantly surprised her, in contrast to her current clients. He pushed his chair back and turned to greet her. Simone's heart plummeted.

"Simone, this is Gabe Harrison. Gabe, Simone Coleman."

The flash of recognition in the guy's eyes matched

her own. The dude at the motorcycle accident scene. Glory Hog was her new client? Hard pass.

Simone looked down at his outstretched hand like it was a poisonous snake.

"Nice to meet you," he murmured. Under his breath, Simone heard him say, "Again."

She briefly touched his hand, pretending to shake it.

"Simone, you may remember Gabe from Main High School. You both went there, right?"

Count on Carson to try to make this little arrangement palatable. Fury rendered her speechless.

Gabe's grin was like a poke from a hot knife. "I'm sure I'd remember if we were in high school at the same time."

Simone resisted the urge to roll her eyes. Glory Hog was also a player.

Carson seemed immune to the tension radiating off her. "When did you say you graduated, Simone?"

Simone spoke through gritted teeth. "2014."

Gabe tapped his chin with his forefinger, no doubt doing some mental calculations. "I graduated in 2011. I would have been a senior when you were a freshman."

"Gee, did you figure that out all by yourself?" Simone couldn't help the sarcasm.

Carson oozed enthusiasm. "You may remember, Gabe led the Dragons to State Championship in baseball that year. He went on to play for Portland State University."

Yeah, Simone remembered. He'd been a glory hog then and he was still a glory hog. She'd had a crush on him for about ten minutes before realizing he was way out of her league. As a senior, it would've been social suicide for him to even glance toward a freshman.

Simone's face grew hot, remembering going to every varsity baseball game with Lizzy. Everyone went to watch their beloved Dragons sweep every team in the league.

She needed to get out of there before Gabe tripped down high school memory lane. "I should get back to my client." She whirled to leave, but Carson stopped her.

"When you're finished, come back to my office and we can work on a plan for my old friend Gabe."

Simone nodded and strode back into the gym. How to get out of Carson's assignment? A male trainer would be better suited for this pariah.

Simone glanced to the ceiling. "Why me, God?" Was he punishing her for being mad that Gabe had gotten all the recognition from saving that guy's life yesterday?

She twirled the purity ring on the ring finger of her left hand as she counted down the last few minutes of Art's time on the bike. Her dad had gifted her the ring on her sixteenth birthday.

"Wear this as a promise to the Lord to remain faithful to him until you get married," he'd said.

Simone had worn the ring until Adam replaced it with a diamond engagement ring. When they'd broken up, Simone had dug the promise ring out of her jewelry box and put it back on.

The way her life was going, she'd probably still be wearing it when she was forty.

Chapter 4

Carson resumed his seat behind his messy desk. "What do you think?"

Gabe pretended ignorance. "About?"

"About Simone. Working with her. Training?" Carson waved a finger in the airs.

Gabe shrugged. "Okay, I guess. How competent is she?"

Carson leaned forward and lowered his voice. "Honestly, she's the best PT I have. I don't know what I'd do without her."

"Hm." Gabe might enjoy working with a female personal trainer. Especially one as hot as Simone. Might be a fun change. But he had doubts that a competent trainer could exist in a town as small as Main. Especially since she'd not only left her phone in the car at the accident scene, and her CPR attempt was pathetic.

Gabe rubbed his chin and feigned ignorance. "Are your employees required to get training in CPR?"

"Of course," Carson responded. "You aren't in danger of a heart attack, are you?" Carson raised his eyebrows with a smirk.

"No." If Simone skated through life-saving training,

how would she treat his training regimen? "When you say she's the best, what are you using as a measurement?"

Carson leaned back and regarded Gabe with narrowed eyes. "What's this about, bro? Are you concerned with Simone's competence?"

"Well—"

"Forget it, Gabe. Simone could leave here tomorrow and have twenty job offers. She's that good."

Gabe wasn't totally convinced, but he let it go. Better to avoid talking about the accident. Carson didn't need to know the guy on the bike would have died if Gabe hadn't shown up.

Carson pulled his laptop close and tapped on the keys. "I'll draw up a contract for you with several options for number of sessions, length of time, and cost. How long will you be here?"

"About four weeks." Gabe's stomach sank. Of course he'd have to sign a contract. He couldn't expect to be trained for free, old friend or not. He'd have to read the fine print to see if there was a cancellation clause.

Carson turned the laptop around. "Read through the agreement and check the box next to the option that works best. Then you can digitally sign it at the bottom."

Gabe shifted in his seat, squirming under Carson's watchful gaze. Sweat prickled under his arms. Carson would no doubt be disappointed to lose his business once Gabe found a facility in Salem. His old friend would want to use Gabe's local celebrity status to build his own clientele.

With reluctance, Gabe agreed to meeting with his

trainer three times a week for two hours. He signed his name, dated the document, and slid the laptop across the desk.

Carson beamed. "Thanks, bro. You won't be sorry. Although you might be sorry once Simone gets her hands on you. Metaphorically speaking."

He'd be facing some sore muscles after the initial few sessions. Since Tiffany, he'd let himself get out of shape. His daily workouts had trickled to maybe once a week. Junk food and lethargy packed on extra pounds he couldn't wait to shed.

This wouldn't be too bad. A pretty personal trainer, Mom's home-cooked food, and some needed time away from the firehouse.

~

Simone dragged out her time with Art, taking longer than usual for his cool down. When Art finally told her he needed to 'skedaddle' back home, she relented and let him go. By the time she arrived back in Carson's office, there was no sign of Glory Hog.

"Where's the g—" Simone gulped. "Your friend."

Carson looked up from his laptop. "He had to get home. You'll start working with him Wednesday. Could you spend some time this afternoon coming up with a training schedule?"

Simone shrugged. "Sure. Anything in particular he's training for, or generally getting back into shape?"

"Ever heard of the 9/11 Memorial Stair Climb?" Simone shook her head. "Have a seat and I'll pull up the website. It's really cool."

Simone sat and waited while Carson tapped his laptop keys. He flipped the screen toward her.

"The 9/11 Memorial Stair Climbs honor FDNY

firefighters who made the ultimate sacrifice. Each 9/11 Memorial Stair Climb participants pays tribute to a FDNY firefighter by climbing or walking the equivalent of the 110 stories of the World Trade Center. Your individual tribute not only remembers the sacrifice of an FDNY brother, but symbolically completes their heroic journey to save others. Through firefighter and community participation we ensure that each of the 343 firefighters is honored and that the world knows that we will never forget."

Simone read and reread the information as a plan began to form. Glory Hog wanted to climb stairs, did he? She mentally rubbed her hands together. She'd give him a workout routine guaranteed to make him beg for mercy.

"I'll see what I can come up with," Simone said.

Until she could work on a plan, she'd work out her frustration on the punching bag. Peeking into the big group exercise room, Simone relaxed a hair when it was empty. She walked across the room to the rack of boxing gloves hanging on the wall. None of the guys would be caught dead in the pink-rimmed gloves and no women had yet to take her up on the offer to train them in the sport of boxing.

The gloves, laced to her exact specifications, slipped easily onto her hands. She punched the gloves together to insure the fit, then went to work on the bag.

One two, one two, pause.

One two, one two, pause.

The heavy bag took the brunt of Simone's pent-up anger and frustration. Dancing around the bag, she feinted right, jabbed, then hit with a left hook. Ten minutes later, sweat dripped down the sides of her face.

Simone wiped off her forehead with the back of one arm. She jumped when Carson spoke behind her.

"I hope I never get into a ring with you, lady. That's quite a punch you've got."

Simone smiled, all traces of her anger gone. "Are you sure, Carson? I'd be happy to go a couple rounds with you."

Carson shook his head with a grimace. "Yeah, no. I value my good looks." He set a finger on his nose. "I wanted to talk with you about our mutual friend, Gabe Harrison."

Simone slapped the gloves together. "What about him?" He's not *my* friend.

Carson shoved his hands in his jean's pockets. "Having a former All-Star train here could mean new business for Gym Time."

Simone regarded her boss with narrowed eyes. "So? Isn't that a good thing?"

"Well, yes, of course. What I'm getting at is . . ."

"Spit it out, Carson. Are you telling me you want to train him yourself?" Simone turned back to the punching bag. "I have no problem if you want to."

Carson reached out to steady the bag when Simone swung a couple more punches. "Uh, no, that's not what I'm saying." He sucked in a breath. "I want to be sure you understand how important it is for Gabe's training to be successful."

Simone swung hard at the bag, practically knocking Carson off balance. Did her boss think she'd phone in Gabe's training? When had she ever let him down? Never. That he'd think she'd skate through the guy's workouts was an insult. She clamped her teeth together to keep from spewing angry words on her boss.

"I have every confidence you'll do a good job. This is a gentle reminder it's important to me Gabe completes the 9/11 challenge. Maybe even show us a little love in the process."

Simone resumed punching. "So noted, Boss."

"You're the best. Thanks."

Simone watched Carson retreat into the main room. When the door clicked closed behind him, she leaned into the hanging bag and rested her forehead on the cool leather. She'd make sure Glory Hog completed the challenge. Or they'd both die in the process.

Chapter 5

Gabe retreated to his room, groaning from another amazing home-cooked meal. At this rate, the fifteen pounds he'd gained would turn into fifty.

"I need to check my emails," he said, dropping a kiss on his mom's cheek.

No email from the fire department in South Carolina. Disappointed, Gabe opened the closet door and reached for a box sitting in the back on the left side. The scrawled black marker on the side read "HS YR books."

He pulled the box off the shelf and heaved it on the bed. Duct tape lay across the top and on each side. Nothing in his desk had been moved or changed since he'd left home. The pair of scissors was still in the top middle drawer. He grabbed them and sliced through the tape.

Crumpled packing paper filled the space between his middle and high school yearbooks and the top of the box. He pulled each one out and smiled, remembering the fun he'd had back when his only responsibilities were keeping up his grades and playing ball.

He laid the six yearbooks on the bed like a fan. The only one he wanted to dive into was from his graduation year. His senior picture showed him looking like a young Ryan Reynolds. With the extra weight he'd gained, his reflection now looked more like Jack Black. He thumbed through until he found the sports team photos toward the back of the yearbook.

His teammates had the sober expressions expected of serious baseball players. Gabe smiled, remembering how they'd tried to get each other to laugh while the photographer set up his equipment. Gabe was among the ones kneeling in front of his team. Carson stood behind him, shoving his knees into the back of Gabe's head, trying to knock him over.

Good times.

Tripping down memory lane was not why he wanted this particular yearbook. He flipped through the pages until he reached the Freshman class. What was Simone's last name? It shouldn't be too hard to find her. She was probably one of the few, if not the only, mixed race girl in her class.

Gabe shook his head. Main was very different from Portland. With a tiny population, Main's largest ethnic group, aside from white, was Mexican. He hoped South Carolina would have the same ethnic diversity that he loved in Portland.

He found Simone's picture easily. Simone Coleman. Her smile revealed braces covering top and bottom and dark hair framed her head in a glorious 'fro. Gabe searched his memory for any indication he'd seen her on campus. None came to mind. Pretty as a freshman, gorgeous as a woman. Calm down. She's out of your league.

Out of curiosity, he turned to the back of the yearbook for the list of clubs. Sure enough, he found

Simone's name under the photo of the on-campus Bible study group.

Gabe slammed the yearbook closed. She was a Christian? Pretty or not, Gabe would have to distance himself from Miss Bible Girl. Definitely out of his league.

"What are you doing, honey?" Gabe's mom stood in the bedroom door. He hadn't heard it open. A burst of heat rose from his belly to his face.

"Uh, doing some reminiscing."

"That's so cute. Let's see."

Mom sat on the bed, pulled Gabe's senior yearbook onto her lap and flipped it open. "Oh, look, here's your friend Carson." Mom pointed to the picture with a smile. "Gosh, you guys look young."

They spent the next thirty minutes laughing over how much everyone had changed in thirteen years. Gabe learned how many of his classmates had moved out of Main and how many still made Main their home.

Mom closed the book with a sigh that spoke volumes.

"What's wrong, Mom?" Mom's forehead furrowed with worry lines.

"I'm worried about your sister. This pregnancy isn't like the other. I wish …"

Gabe waited, but his mom didn't continue. She placed the yearbook on the bed and struggled to her feet. "I better go see how your dad is doing with the girls."

Gabe wished there was something he could do to erase the creases on his mom's face.

~

After an evening spent researching the September

11 memorial stair climb, Simone had a good handle on how to get Glory Hog into shape. She emailed the detailed thirty-day plan to Carson. Thinking about Carson brought on a wave of irritation. Hadn't she given her best to this job, day in and day out, working with difficult clients that Carson didn't want?

Once Glory Hog's training was finished, Simone would add it to her resume. If the guy completed the challenge, that is. It was a grueling event for even the most in shape men and women. Glory Hog looked like he hadn't missed a Super-sized meal in weeks.

She had her work cut out for her.

After her morning Bible reading, Simone spent a few minutes praying for her family. A twinge of prompting by the Holy Spirit reminded her to pray for the man from the motorcycle accident. Today she'd see if he was still in the hospital. She shook her head, remembering how scared she'd been he wouldn't respond to CPR.

Which reminded her of Glory Hog. No, God, I can't pray for him.

Yes, you can.

Simone sighed and spoke aloud. "Fine. Bless Glory Hog today. And make sure he survives the training I have set out for him."

Simone arrived at Gym Time early enough to do a few exercises before Carson wandered in.

"Did you look at the schedule I sent you for your friend?"

Carson nodded with a yawn. "Looks good."

Simone ground her teeth. She'd spent at least two hours of her own time creating a plan Glory Hog may not be able to complete, and all her boss could say was 'looks good?' Another reason to look for another job.

Carson made his way to his office, Simone at his heels. He set his Yeti coffee mug on the desk.

"I have a couple of interviews today for the admin position. Want to sit in with me?"

Simone scratched her nose. "Why?" Carson had never asked her opinion before hiring anyone.

"I thought you might give a woman's perspective, since both applicants are female."

"Can I let you know?" Simone needed to think through his offer. If he hired someone who didn't work out, she'd probably be blamed.

Carson took a sip of his beverage and nodded. "Gabe will be here tomorrow to get started on his training."

Simone raised herself up on her toes and back down. "Okay."

Good. She had a day without having to be reminded of Glory Hog. The rest of the day passed in a blur. A text came in as Simone was gathering her things to go home.

Mariah: Can you two meet me for coffee? Need to talk wedding.

Simone responded with a thumbs up and hoped Lizzy was available too. Simone wasn't mentally prepared to contend with Mariah's strong will. The last thing she wanted was to be forced into helping plan Mariah's wedding. With Lizzy there to act as a buffer, she'd be safe from Mariah's schemes. Or so she hoped.

Lizzy breezed into Cookie's Cafe a few minutes after Simone and Mariah.

"Sorry I'm late."

"No problem." Mariah took a delicate sip from her water, then wiped the condensation on a napkin.

Simone wondered for the millionth time how the woman was able to keep her lipstick on without a smear. Simone usually swiped the mascara wand over her lashes and called it good. Any makeup would get sweated or wiped off during her day.

Mariah reached into her red leather bag and pulled out her iPad. "I made some notes and I wanted to run them by you." Glancing up, she added, "My bridesmaids."

"Are we the only two?" Simone asked. She wasn't sure if she was relieved or alarmed that Mariah had chosen to have only two bridesmaids.

"You guys are it. I've created a spreadsheet for each of you."

Simone's empty stomach shriveled to the size of a raisin.

Count on Mariah to have everything planned to the nth degree.

"Oh, great," Lizzy said.

Simone searched her friend's face for sarcasm. Finding none, she added. "Yeah. Great."

As Mariah went on to explain what their duties were, Simone's attention turned to the program she had in store for the guy she called Glory Hog.

"Are you even listening?" Mariah's exasperated voice interrupted her musings.

"Uh …"

"I knew it," Mariah said, setting her iPad on the table with more force than was necessary.

Simone tried for an attitude of apology. "Sorry. I have a lot on my mind."

Ever the peacemaker, Lizzy spoke up. "What's going on, Simone. You can tell us."

Simone sucked in a breath, then exhaled. "Remember when I saw that guy take a spill on his motorcycle? And how that glory hog guy got all the credit?"

"I remember. Are you still stewing over that? You need to let it go," Mariah said.

Simone's heart sped up, remembering how the motorcycle swerved off the road and flipped in the weeds.

"Who's the guy on the bike and is he okay?" Lizzy asked.

Simone shrugged. "I don't know how to find out."

Mariah tapped a pink tipped fingernail on the Formica table. "Maybe you can ask at the fire station. If this glory hog guy is one of them, it shouldn't be too hard to find him."

Simone frowned, remembering how the guy had eyed her up and down in Carson's office.

"I know who he is. His name is Gabe Harrison. He went to Main High."

Mariah gasped. "Gabriel Harrison, the baseball All-Star?"

"The same."

Her friends went silent as they exchanged glances.

Simone heaved a sigh. "That's not all. Glory Hog is my new client at the gym."

Chapter 6

Gabe wiped sweat from his brow and jumped off the tractor.

"Thanks, Dad, for giving me the afternoon off to train."

"I'm proud of you, Son, for wanting to remember your fallen comrades."

Gabe basked in his dad's praise. He'd enjoy his father's approval while it lasted. Hopefully, his parents would never know what a dumpster fire his life had become.

"Look out there, Gabe," Dad said, pointing to the waving stalks of grass. "We've been providing grass for athletic fields and golf courses for over fifty years." Dad's eyes misted. "I'd hoped you'd want to take over when I'm ready to retire. But I understand your desire to do your own thing."

Gabe's lungs constricted with guilt. His escape plan from Main included college in Portland and a job in a big fire department. Main, Oregon was too small for his big dreams.

How long could Mom and Dad run the farm? Would they be forced to sell off part of the hundred or so acres to stay in his childhood home?

Gabe headed into the house with a heavy heart. The stinging spray of a cool shower washed away some of his gloom. Thinking about the upcoming training session cheered him up.

What would the lovely personal trainer have for him today? He hoped it would be an easy workout for the first day.

He changed into athletic shorts and a tee shirt that fit a little more tightly than he wanted. Running a hand down his stomach, he cringed at the extra girth. After this next month of training, he'd be back in top physical shape.

If Simone was everything Carson had said, that is.

Before leaving the house, Gabe peeked into his sister's bedroom to say goodbye. Finding the bed empty, he went in search of the woman who was supposed to be taking it easy.

Gabe found his mom in the kitchen, making iced tea. "Mom, have you seen Gracie?"

"She's outside with Mercy and Hope."

Gabe charged out the back door, intending to give his sister a lecture about taking care of herself. He found her in the shade of an oak tree on a padded lounger. The twins splashed and played in a wading pool nearby.

"You're supposed to be on bedrest," Gabe exclaimed.

Grace lowered her sunglasses to peer at him. "What do you think I'm doing?"

Gabe sputtered a response. "B-but I thought—"

"Relax, little brother. As long as I take it easy, the doctor said it was okay to go outside. Don't worry, I'm not planning to high dive into the wading pool." She sent him a grin.

Relief poured off him as he grinned back. "You look ready to pop," he said, pointing at her belly, swelling under her tank top.

"I'm ready to pop. Five more weeks, or so the doctor says. As long as I stay calm and don't exert myself, I should be able to go full term."

Gabe put his hands on his hips. "Don't get any ideas about going into labor when I'm here. I've only watched how to deliver a baby on YouTube."

Grace laughed, then cringed. "Oh, don't make me laugh. I'll have to go pee and I'm comfy here."

"On that note, I'm outta here." Gabe turned to go, sending an air kiss to his nieces.

~

Simone's nerves ratcheted up when she saw the white pickup pull into the gym parking lot. She was filled with grim satisfaction with the torture she planned to inflict on the guy who dared to steal all the attention from the motorcycle accident.

It was all anyone could talk about at the gym. Simone had even heard rumors of a City Council recognition of what they called their Hometown Hero.

She gritted her teeth, still feeling the shoulders of the paramedics who had shoved her out of the way.

No time to dwell on it now. Simone had a job to do, and she'd show her boss she was capable of taking Glory Hog to 9/11 memorial success.

Gabe strode into the gym without casting a glance her way. He headed straight to Carson's office. Simone navigated through the machines, stopping to help here and there.

"Try keeping your arms at shoulder level when you

do the lift," Simone said to one. To another, she said, "Good form, Bart. Try adding a bit more weight next time, okay?"

She reached Carson's office and stopped outside, listening to his and Gabe's conversation.

Carson's voice carried over the music pumped in through the gym speakers. "Your workout plan looks intense. You sure you're ready for this?"

"Yup. I need to get back into shape. I kind of let myself go after some personal stuff went down."

Hm. What personal stuff could Glory Hog be dealing with? His life appeared to be perfect. Great reputation here in Main, all his education paid for with a baseball scholarship, parents who were still married, and a great job in Portland. What could have caused a little blip in his perfect life?

Someone called out to her from the gym, so Simone missed the next part of the conversation. After she finished helping a woman change the intensity of the treadmill, Carson and Glory Hog were coming out of Carson's office.

"There you are," Carson said. "Gabe is ready to get started."

Gabe strode toward her with a grin. He wouldn't be grinning very much longer.

"Let's get warmed up," Simone said, leading him into the big workout room. A yoga class was being held on one side, so Simone pulled some mats off the rack and laid them on the floor on the other side of the room.

She led her new client through some warmup stretches. "Are you ready to begin?" she asked when their muscles were suitably warm.

"Sure. Let's get this party started."

Simone led Gabe outside. "C'mon, let's go." She started off down the sidewalk with an easy jog.

Gabe caught up a couple of seconds later. "Why are we running?"

Simone glanced at him out of the corner of her eye. "We need to increase your lung capacity to enable you to make the climb. Right now, you look a little soft. Tell me about your workout routine."

He'd probably tell her about how much weight he could bench press or how many reps of curls he could do with heavy hand weights. Instead, he didn't say anything.

~

Gabe's breath came in short puffs. This lady wanted to talk and all he wanted to do was try to suck air into his burning lungs.

"Did you not hear me?" Simone asked as they turned the corner and headed toward City Hall.

"Yeah," he huffed. "I heard you." Gabe hated the way his voice sounded—like he was gargling his lungs.

"This'll be an easy jog. Around City Hall, past the Police Department, and back to the gym. It's about a mile."

Gabe thanked God for the shortness of the run. He could gut it out for a mile. He sent a grin toward his trainer, hoping it didn't look like a grimace.

Simone quirked an eyebrow at him. "We'll do it five times."

Gabe stumbled, then righted himself. Five miles? She had to be kidding. A quick glance showed she was not kidding. In fact, she seemed to be enjoying herself.

Sweat soon soaked Gabe's shirt. It clung to his back like a hot blanket.

He could barely hear her voice over his pulse pounding in his ears.

"There's nothing like running outside," Simone said. "Running on the treadmill is fine when it's raining, but this," she spread out an arm to the trees hanging over the sidewalk. "This is amazing. God's creation in all its glory."

Gabe couldn't focus on God's creation because of the sweat stinging his eyes.

Simone went on talking as if she were standing still. "The lungs are an amazing part of our bodies. Their main job is to move fresh air in and push waste gases out. The lungs are the centerpiece of the respiratory system. But the only way to increase their capacity is to exercise them. I'll bet you don't know how many alveoli your lungs have."

At that point, Gabe couldn't have cared less how many of anything. His alveoli burned, along with every muscle in his legs.

Simone continued, "Your lungs have about 150 million alveoli. They're able to expand and contract, helping the lungs inflate and deflate. Cool, huh?"

The rest of Simone's chatter became white noise. His brain shut off somewhere around the second lap. Gabe questioned his life choices, his lack of exercise, and wondered why he'd not only agreed to this torture but was paying for the experience.

When they finally returned to the parking lot of Gym Time, Gabe's legs felt like blocks of concrete. He leaned forward, resting his hands on his thighs and wheezed in and out.

"Too much for you, Glory Hog?" Simone asked.

Gabe tilted his head up. "Glory Hog?"

Simone didn't answer. She spun on her heels and opened the door to the gym. A blast of cold air hit Gabe's overheated face.

"You better get some water or a sports drink," Simone said, disappearing into the gym.

Gabe limped after her and headed into the men's restroom to splash water on his face. He dried his face with a rough paper towel and regarded himself in the mirror. "Glory Hog?" he said aloud.

Chapter 7

Simone felt a tiny sliver of guilt over making the guy run five miles on his first day. But the memory of how he'd let everyone pat him on the back and high five him at the accident scene squashed any sympathy.

She strode into the front office and retrieved two flavored sports drinks from the refrigerator. She'd have Carson put them on her tab. She returned to the main gym and shoved one of the drinks in Gabe's direction.

"Drink up and then we'll do some cool down."

Gabe screwed off the top of the plastic bottle and chugged down half the cold liquid. "Thanks," he said, wiping his mouth with the back of one hand.

"Come with me." She led Gabe into the big workout room where their mats still lay on the floor. She led him through a series of stretches.

"When you get home, take a hot shower right away. Don't let lactic acid build up in your muscles or you'll be sore tomorrow."

Gabe nodded.

"If you are sore, take some ibuprofen or Motrin. If you've got a hot tub at home, try soaking for twenty minutes tonight."

Gabe sent her a mock salute. "Anything else?"

Simone regarded him with steely eyes. "Are you sure you want to go through with this training? Four weeks isn't very long for such a rigorous challenge." Simone hoped she'd scared the guy enough to back out when he had the chance. She didn't want to admit she was impressed he'd made the five-mile run without stopping. Besides, she was a sucker for a guy with good legs. And Glory Hog had amazing legs.

Gabe grinned at her from where he lay on his back on the mat. "Are you trying to get rid of me?"

That's exactly what I'm trying to do.

"Of course not. I'm merely concerned that you won't make it up a hundred ten stories in your current condition." Simone shrugged as if it was a foregone conclusion he'd withdraw.

Gabe raised himself up on his elbows. "It's your job to ensure my current condition becomes my future condition."

Simone swallowed the words she wanted to rain down on him. Talk about ego. "Then don't expect to be pampered, Glory."

"What's with the moniker?"

Simone rolled her eyes. "Think about it. I started CPR on the guy on the bike. You came along and took over, then grabbed all the attention for saving the guy's life."

Gabe had the audacity to lay back on the mat and guffaw. "That's what this is about? You're upset because no one complimented you on forgetting your phone in your car? What did you think, that you'd continue to work on the victim until someone happened along?"

Simone hadn't thought that through. But this wasn't

the time to admit it. "Look. Let's agree to disagree on this. If I hadn't seen the guy go off the road, he'd still by lying in the field." Simone gulped. "Dead."

Gabe struggled to his feet and stood facing her. Simone noticed the unusual color of his brown eyes. Like unsweet tea. His sweat had dried, and the University of Portland tee shirt clung to his frame. Even with the extra pounds he carried, Simone could tell there were muscles underneath. She took a step back, suddenly aware of his maleness. When had the room shrunk?

"Your session is over for today." Simone spun around and headed for the door. "See you Friday."

She strode through the gym and headed to the front reception area, creating as much distance as possible from Gabe. Great legs or not, she had a job to do and a month to do it. She would not let herself be attracted to someone like Gabe.

~

Gabe's sister told him once that women don't sweat. They glow. His trainer was definitely glowing. He took another gulp of his drink as Simone retreated from the workout room. The dryness of his mouth had less to do with the five-mile run and more to do with the woman herself.

Despite her antagonism, Gabe couldn't help notice how pretty she was. No, pretty was the wrong word. She had an exotic beauty, reminding him of a photo he'd once seen of the famous twins Tia and Tamera Mowry.

The woman was feisty, and he liked that. Gabe rubbed a hand across his face. Back it down, cowboy. Getting involved with a woman wasn't in the plan.

He'd be leaving in a month and Simone wasn't an entanglement he needed. Tiffany's betrayal still burned. How could he enjoy another relationship when he'd been a part of creating and then destroying an innocent life?

Gabe hopped in his pickup and pointed it toward his parents' house. What to do about finding a personal trainer in the larger city of Salem? It would mean at least thirty minutes, maybe more, to get there. Could he spare that kind of time when he only had four weeks to train?

On the other hand, could he keep emotional distance from the lovely Simone while working closely with her for the next month? Yes, he could. Maybe.

After dinner, his mom took Grace's girls into the bathroom for a bath.

"Come sit with me," his sister implored. "I need some adult company."

Gabe pulled a chair up to the side of her bed. "Want to play cards?"

Grace narrowed her eyes. "As long as you don't cheat."

Gabe placed a hand on his chest. "Me? Cheat? I don't have to cheat to beat you, Sis."

"Ha. Go get the TV tray from the living room. And bring the cards."

Gabe's dad snoozed in his recliner in the living room. Fox News was on and the talking heads predicted dire circumstances coming soon. As usual. He turned the volume down.

He returned to his sister's room with a deck of cards and the requested TV tray. "What's your pleasure?" he asked, splitting the deck in half and shuffling it.

Grace leaned forward with a groan and reached behind her to fluff her pillows. "Do you remember how to play Cribbage?"

Gabe nodded. "Sure. Let me grab the Cribbage board."

He found the board in the game closet behind a stack of jigsaw puzzles. Maybe he and Grace could put one of them together. They'd spent hours of time as kids seeing who could get the most pieces added to the puzzle in the shortest amount of time.

Everything had been a competition back then. Which of them could jump the farthest. Who made the biggest splash from the high dive in the community pool. Who had the most wins in their card games.

Now that he was back home, he could use his competitive skills to accomplish everything he needed to do. Help his dad, watch out for his sister, and prove to himself that he had what it took to complete the September 11 stair challenge.

"You ready to lose to the master?" Gabe asked, setting the Cribbage board on the tray.

"You wish," Grace responded.

The arrival of Grace's twins interrupted their second game. They hopped on the bed to give their mom sloppy kisses, talking over each other.

"Give your mom some space," Gabe's mom warned.

"It's fine, Mom. I miss my babies." Grace pulled her girls in, one on each side. Gabe marveled at their perfect blend of his sister's light hair and fair complexion, and their dad's darker skin.

Gabe remembered when Grace brought Demarcus home to meet the family. They'd taught Grace and

Gabe that God doesn't look at the outward appearance, but on the heart. His parents had taken only a moment to welcome Demarcus as their future son-in-law.

As Gabe watched the girls cuddle with his sister, he was reminded of Simone's obvious mixed-race heritage. Had her parents faced some of the challenges Grace and Demarcus had faced? Sometimes small-town people carried prejudice that transcended Biblical teaching. Even in the church, Gabe sometimes found racism running rampant.

It wasn't until he'd left Main for college in Portland that he'd discovered how diverse a community could be.

He shoved the thoughts of the lovely Simone out of his mind. The twins leaned in for a goodnight kiss from their uncle. He grabbed each of them and tickled them until they squealed.

"Nice job, little brother. Get them all hyped up before bed." Grace crossed her arms and frowned.

"Sorry." He wasn't sorry. He loved those munchkins and hoped someday to have one of his own. Unless God had other plans. The big guy upstairs was probably disappointed in Gabe's life choices.

What had he seen in Tiffany, anyway? She turned out to be someone he didn't even like. That she'd carelessly toss away her baby—their baby—grieved him still.

His inattention to their game gave his sister an easy win. "That's two for me, little bro," she crowed. "Want to go best of five?"

Gabe tossed his cards on the TV tray. "I think I'll head to bed. I'm beat."

Grace grinned at him. "How was your workout?"

'Brutal."

"You're working with Carson at Gym Time, right?"

Gabe nodded. "Yeah. Gym Time."

"I always liked Carson. Even back in high school, he was a nice guy. I wonder why he's never gotten married."

Gabe gathered the cards and slid them into their box. "I have no idea. Guys don't talk about stuff like that."

Grace laughed. "Oh, yeah, I forgot. Guys never gossip." She rolled her eyes. "What's he like as a personal trainer? I've heard good things about him."

Gabe felt himself grow warm. "I'm, uh, not actually working with Carson."

"Really? Who's your trainer? Is it anyone I know?"

"Have you always been this nosy?" Gabe got to his feet and picked up the cards and Cribbage board.

"Come on, Gabe. I'm lying here all day, bored out of my mind. Can't you throw me a bone? A little tiny crumb of information? Please?"

Gabe couldn't help but smile down at her pitiful expression. "Her name is Simone Coleman."

Grace raised her eyes to the ceiling. "Hm, I don't think I know her. Did she grow up here?"

"Main High School, class of 2014."

"Ah. That was way after me. Did you know her in school?"

Gabe shook his head. "She was a freshman when I was a senior." He leaned down to plant a kiss on Grace's forehead. "Good night, Sis. Sleep well."

Grace crossed her arms and glared. "You better give me more deets tomorrow, mister."

Gabe sent her a grin and a salute. "Yes, ma'am."

Chapter 8

Thursday morning brought the promise of another perfect summer day. With no clients on her roster, Simone sent a text to Carson.

Taking the day off.

Next stop, Salem and her favorite grocery store.

She sent a quick text to Lizzy.

Heading to Trader Joes. Want anything?

Lizzy shared Simone's addiction to everything Trader Joes. Lizzy sent an immediate response.

Lizzy: Yes, please!!! Get me one of those broccoli kale chicken salads. No, make that two. And some of those chocolate-covered almonds. Milk, not dark. That way I don't have to share with R.

Simone smiled. Salad and chocolate. A perfect combination.

After a quick stop at the folks', Simone turned her car toward home. Simone sped over the Marion Bridge, grateful no accidents had caused a traffic jam like on Sunday. Her mind returned to the accident with the motorcyclist. What would she have done if Glory Hog hadn't come along? Would she have continued CPR until her arms collapsed? What if Gabe hadn't stopped? What an idiot she was for leaving her phone charging in the car.

But Gabe had stopped. Despite the adrenaline surging through her veins at the time, Simone had noticed the guy's killer looks. Too bad he was such a jerk. Four weeks and he'd scurry back to wherever he came from, and she'd be rid of him. If he completed the stair challenge, she'd add that to her resume and seriously look for another job.

Simone could only hope if he did complete the challenge and got some media attention, that he'd share some of the glory with his personal trainer.

Probably not. Ergh. Like back in high school, once a glory hog, always a glory hog.

The *whoop whoop* of a state trooper's siren pulled her attention to the rearview mirror. A shot of adrenaline hit when she glanced at her speedometer. Uh oh. She'd been going close to seventy in the fifty-five-mile zone.

She slowed her Honda and signaled to pull over, the trooper glued on her tail.

When the officer approached the passenger side of her car, Simone rolled down the window, letting in a blast of afternoon heat.

"Good afternoon, Ma'am. I pulled you over because I clocked you at seventy-one. License, insurance, and registration please."

"I'm sorry, Officer. I was distracted."

The trooper's hands rested on his belt while he waited for Simone to fumble in the glove box for the envelope holding her registration and insurance card. She handed them to the officer, along with her driver's license.

"Here you go."

"Simone Coleman?" His voice held surprise.

Simone squinted at the name tag on his left breast. "Monty?"

He pulled off his sunglasses with a grin. "It's Carl now. No one calls me Monty anymore."

"Oh my gosh! It's great to see you. When did you move back?"

Monty, no, Carl leaned down and rested his forearms on the car door. "I've been back about two weeks."

"That's awesome. I'll bet your folks are glad."

His face clouded over. "Yeah, my dad has early onset dementia and I wanted to be closer to help my mom out. How about your parents?"

Simone shrugged. "Same old same old." Too much drama to elaborate.

"I hear ya." Carl gave her an appraising look. "You look the same as you did in high school."

"I can't say the same about you." Carl had been a skinny geek in high school. Now he was a lot taller and had filled out nicely. Simone's eyes were drawn to the well-defined biceps peeking out from his uniform shirt.

"Say, Simone. A bunch of us are getting together for the first outdoor concert of the season tomorrow night. Why don't you join us?"

Simone didn't hesitate. She loved Main's Hot August Nights concert series. Exceptional music, the best ice cream in the world, and reconnecting with seldom-seen friends. "I'd like that."

"Great. I'll pick you up, say around six? I have your address." He waved her license.

"Uh, sure. I guess that'd be okay." Might be nice to have a date after Adam's abrupt departure.

"All right. It's a date then." Carl handed her license back, along with the registration and insurance cards. "I'm not going to give you a ticket. That would not be a good start to our relationship. But slow down, okay? I'd hate to see you get in an accident." Carl double-tapped the roof of her Honda before turning and striding back to his patrol car.

Simone heaved a sigh of relief. She'd never gotten a speeding ticket before. Even with her lead foot on the accelerator, she'd been lucky. But what had Carl said? 'A start to their relationship'?

Could she get involved in another relationship so soon after her breakup with Adam? A mental image of Gabe pushed its way into her thoughts. She shoved it away.

Nope. Glory Hog would soon be past history. Maybe Carl would be her future. At least until she found another job.

At her apartment, Simone carried the box she'd retrieved from her parents' attic from the back seat of her Honda. She set it on the kitchen table and found the box cutter in the junk drawer.

The tape slit easily, and she was soon pulling old yearbooks and photos from the box. When she found the one from her senior year, Simone sank onto a chair and flipped it open. There was Carl "Monty" Montgomery in his senior gown, squinting through thick, black-framed glasses. He'd either gotten contact lenses or laser surgery since graduation. He looked a lot better as a grown man than he did as a skinny, geeky high schooler.

Simone hadn't paid much attention to Monty in school. That was about to change.

Morbid curiosity made her dig through the box for her freshman year. She paused at her yearbook photo long enough to cringe. Those braces! That awful kinky hair.

She flipped through the classes until coming to the senior class. Of course, Gabe's photo showed him as a handsome eighteen-year-old. Like a young Ryan Reynolds or maybe Brad Pitt. No wonder he'd been out of her league. To think she'd had a crush on him.

Ugh.

She slammed the book closed. That was then and this was now.

Simone twirled her promise ring and prayed for wisdom.

~

Gabe changed into his workout clothes with a sense of anticipation. What would Simone torture him with today? More running? Ugh. He hoped not. Running was his least favorite form of exercise. Give him some weights and he'd be happy.

He stuck his head in his sister's bedroom door and bade her goodbye. "Be good, Sis. Don't give Mom any trouble."

She looked up from the book she was reading and stuck out her tongue. "Still the annoying little brother."

"Guilty as charged," Gabe said, heading for the front door.

The sound of his dad's combine rumbled in the distance. Mom had put the twins down for a nap and was helping Dad in the field for an hour or two until the girls woke up. The smell of freshly turned dirt filled the air. The smell of his childhood. Gabe breathed deeply of the earthy scent, remembering the hours he'd spent working on the farm and hating every moment. Now he wished he could recapture some of those times. The past always seemed better than the present.

Oh well, he had this new thing to take his mind off Tiffany. He'd concentrate on the upcoming stair challenge and hope to shove her into the dark recesses of his brain.

Gabe strode into Gym Time with a light step. He stopped inside the door and watched Simone as she helped an older woman with one of the machines. Her chin-length hair swung over her cheek as she leaned down to listen to the woman. His breath caught for a moment until he remembered why he was here.

To train. Not to be attracted to his trainer.

Right.

Simone looked up and their eyes met. She immediately looked away. Was he that repulsive that she couldn't hold eye contact for more than a millisecond? Yeah, he'd puffed up a bit over the past several months. Still . . .

"Hey, buddy." Carson's voice sounded in Gabe's ear. "She's something to look at, right?"

"Uh, yeah, she's all right I guess."

Carson slapped him on the back. "She's more than all right. I'd ask her out if she wasn't working for me." Carson shook his head in mock regret. "Maybe I should fire her . . ." he shrugged.

Gabe forced out a laugh. "Like that would make her want to go out with you. 'You're fired. Wanna have dinner?' I don't think so, dude." Gabe shoved down a sliver of jealousy. Why would he feel jealous over Carson's obvious attraction to Simone?

The woman herself approached the two men. "You

ready, Glory?"

Carson raised his eyebrows. "Glory?"

Simone's mouth turned down. "Long story. Your friend, here will have to tell you all about it."

She grabbed Gabe's arm and pulled him away from Carson. Gabe sent Carson an apologetic look before letting himself be dragged into the large, empty workout room.

"Today we're going to do some circuit training," Simone explained. "I've set up five stations around the room. You'll do each exercise for one minute, then move onto the next after a thirty-second rest."

Gabe glanced around the room. "No running today?"

Simone sent him an evil grin. "That'll be afterwards."

Gabe huffed out a sigh. Better get this shindig started. "Where do I begin?"

Simone walked him around to all the stations, explaining what he'd be doing at each one. Medicine ball squats, bosu ball pushups, wall sit holding the medicine ball out in front, exercise band pull-ups using his body weight, and jump rope.

"Are you ready?" Simone asked. She held a timer in one hand.

"Shouldn't I warm up first?"

Simone rolled her eyes. "I thought you'd already be warmed up." She moved to the center of the room. "Let's go through some basic stretches.

Gabe watched Simone out of the corner of his eye, admiring the way her leggings hugged her slim legs. A guy could watch without being attracted, right?

Keep telling yourself that, dude.

"Okay, let's get started," Simone said, striding toward the first station. "You remember how to do this?" She handed him the heavy medicine ball as if weighed no more than a balloon.

He held it to his chest and waited for her signal to begin.

Forty minutes later, his shirt was soaked and his breath came in short gasps.

"Let's check your heart rate," Simone said, grabbing his wrist.

Gabe's skin burned where her two fingers lay on his wrist. He stared down at the tiny diamond ring on her left hand. She was engaged? Why did that bother him so much? He remembered Carson's off-hand comment about wanting to date Simone, but he never mentioned anything about a fiancé. Gabe never pictured Carson as a player.

"What do you do for fun around here?" Gabe asked.

"Sh. I'm trying to get your pulse. Now I have to start over."

Gabe didn't mind letting Simone continue to grasp his wrist. Her fingers were long and tapered into short nails. No polish. He flashed back to Tiffany's talon-like fingernails before shoving the memory back where it belonged.

Simone dropped his wrist and walked over to where she'd laid her iPad. Gabe watched as she made some notations.

"What's the verdict?" he asked.

"One sixty. That's a little high for what you've been doing. I'd like to see it around one forty. Do you happen to know your baseline?" She was all business. Gabe wanted to take their conversation into a more personal level.

"You didn't answer my question," Gabe said.

Simone looked up at him with a frown. "You didn't answer mine."

"No, I don't remember my baseline heart rate." He waited a beat. "What do you do for fun around here?"

"Let's go outside and take a couple of laps." Simone set the iPad on a shelf and turned her back toward him.

Gabe sighed. He'd had better luck with women in the past. Why was this one seemingly immune to his charm?

Simone started them out with a slow jog. As his feet pounded on the sidewalk, Gabe wondered if Simone was one of those women who only looked at the outward appearance of a guy. There was a verse in the Bible about that.

She's engaged, he reminded himself.

Why had he not noticed the ring before?

"Are you familiar with adipose tissue?" Simone asked on their second lap around City Hall.

"Are they the newest alternative rock band?" Gabe's attempt at humor fell flat. Simone's frown confirmed it.

"Adipose tissue is that extra weight you're carrying around your gut."

Gabe wished he'd fall in a hole and disappear. All those loaded burritos sat heavily around his middle. Simone probably looked at him like a fat, ugly couch potato.

Simone continued, oblivious to Gabe's embarrassment. "Adipose tissue is found under your skin, between your internal organs. Know how to get rid of it?"

How did the woman run and talk at the same time? Gabe's lungs burned. Or rather, his alveoli burned like a wildfire in the Oregon wilderness.

"Exercise," Simone said. "Exercise activates the hormone irisin, which tells white fat in your body to burn."

Gabe grunted. Simone's amused grin irritated him more than he cared to admit. He increased his pace until he ran in front of her. They rounded the corner to Gym Time. Gabe didn't look to see how far behind Simone was. Let her keep up with him for a change. As he passed Henry's Boutique, he glanced to his left at his reflection in the store windows. He didn't see Simone behind him. Had he run too fast for her?

Gabe stopped and turned. Simone stood back at the corner, arms crossed over her chest. He raised his arms in a 'what's up?' motion.

"We're only doing two laps today," Simone yelled.

Gabe bit down hard on his bottom lip to keep from cursing. That woman would be the death of him. Literally.

Chapter 9

Simone glanced at the time on her phone and hoped she'd be ready for Monty. Oops, Carl. The sunny day had turned into a partially cloudy afternoon, typical of a Main summer evening. The forecast promised no rain until midnight.

She set her phone on the dresser and put it on speaker. Lizzy's voice boomed through the device. "What are you going to wear on your date with Carl?"

Simone stared into her closet with a frown. "I'm trying to figure that out now."

"Is this your first date since, you know, that guy whose name we don't mention."

Simone chuckled. "Yes, it is. You remember he was Monty the Geek in high school. Well now he's Carl the cop."

Lizzy snorted. "That's funny. I always thought he was kinda cute."

"You would. Look who you're married to."

"Hey, don't dis my man."

"Whatever." Simone pulled a pair of jeans off a hanger. It always felt weird to wear something other than yoga pants or workout leggings.

"We need to go clothes shopping for you," Lizzy

said. "You're probably staring into your closet trying to find something to wear. Am I right?"

Simone tossed the jeans on the bed with a sigh. "You're right."

"I better go. Abby is making noises about starving to death."

"Love you."

"Call me tomorrow and tell me how it went."

Simone disconnected and reached for a tee shirt that was slightly dressier than her usual work clothes. She added a sweatshirt, tying it around her waist. Once the sun dropped behind the trees, the temperature would dip.

Nerves skittered up Simone's back as she waited for Carl to pick her up. Lizzy was right, Simone hadn't been on a date since her breakup with Adam. After their year-long engagement, Adam accepted a job in Nevada without consulting her. Simone still felt the sting of betrayal. Adam knew she couldn't leave Oregon. She was tied to her parents and her little sister. That had been a source of contention in their relationship.

Simone shoved the closet door. No sense in dwelling on the past. Time to go out and have some fun with Carl and listen to some good music.

Carl knocked on her apartment door at exactly six o'clock. He opened the passenger door of his car and waited for Simone to get settled before closing it. His sedan smelled like fresh laundry and was as clean.

Carl climbed in and buckled his seatbelt. "Ready?"

A blue short-sleeve buttoned shirt fit nicely around his chest. He wore dark jeans and a pair of nondescript tennis shoes.

Carl kept up a running dialog on the short drive to

the outdoor concert venue.

"Remember when some kids sprinkled laundry soap on the football field? When it rained, it foamed up like snow."

Simone laughed. "Did they ever figure out who did it?"

"Nope." He leaned toward her. "I have my suspicions, but no one has 'fessed up."

They passed Main hospital. "That's new since I left," Carl said, pointing at the addition to the Emergency Room. "And that over there used to be the Catholic Church. Looks like a homeless shelter now." He frowned.

"The church moved to a new building on the highway." Simone knew a handful of people who attended Mass.

Carl pulled into the police department lot and placed a placard on the dash. "One of the benefits of the job."

"I'll bet," Simone said. "I usually drive around downtown several times looking for a parking spot." If she didn't get there early, she'd end up parking several blocks away.

"I'll get your door," Carl said when Simone reached for the handle.

She waited while he got out and came around to her side of the car. He held out a hand to help her out.

Carl closed the door but didn't release Simone's hand. She bit the inside of her cheek, trying to decide if it was too intimate for a first date or if it was sweet. The music became louder as they neared the stage.

"Some of our old high school buddies will be here too," Carl told her. "This is gonna be fun."

"I love these concerts. I try to go every week during August to listen to music and hang out with friends." It was nice to not have to attend alone this year. She'd asked Lizzy to go, but she said it was too uncomfortable to sit on a hard chair or on the ground for a couple of hours in her condition. Mariah said she and Ethan might go, depending on if they could find someone to watch Ethan's son Jayden.

Carl pointed to a group of people standing to one side of the venue. "There they are." He pulled Simone toward them, increasing his pace until they reached the group.

Simone stopped short when she saw Glory Hog standing with a group of her former high school friends. What was he doing here? Was he one of the ones Carl had invited? Now she'd be forced to make nice with the guy.

Gabe caught her eye and sent her a lazy grin. His eyes narrowed when his gaze dropped to hers and Carl's clasped hands. Simone resisted the urge to pull away from Carl.

Who cares what he thinks? Not me.

The greetings were boisterous and laughter-filled as the young men and women got reacquainted. Their ages spanned from a few months to a few years, but the gap seemed irrelevant now that they were all adults.

"You all remember Simone, right?" Carl was saying.

Gabe stepped forward. "Of course, I remember Simone," he said. His expression challenged her to argue.

Simone clamped her jaws together as Gabe continued. "Didn't you have a mouthful of braces in high school? And it seems like I remember your awesome 'fro."

Simone vowed to kill him at their next workout. She'd let her hair get wild during her teenage years, trying to embrace her African American heritage. Only later when she was at college did she let her hair grow out. She spent time every week using a flat iron to straighten it.

Gabe's comment brought a titter of laughter to the group. Simone was saved from having to respond by Mariah's appearance.

"Hey everyone." She moved in to hug Simone.

"Hey, girl, glad you made it," Simone said.

Carl's eyes widened and he raised his eyebrows. "Mariah Martin?"

Mariah sent him a dazzling smile. "That's right, Monty. Let me introduce you to my fiancé, Ethan Walsh."

While Ethan shook hands and was introduced, Carl grabbed Simone's hand again and pulled her a few feet away.

"I didn't know you were friends with Mean Mariah."

Simone's slow anger over Gabe now flamed into fury. "Don't call her that. Mariah is my friend."

"Whoa, slow down. I didn't mean anything by it. I'm surprised. She and her little posse made my life miserable back in school. I thought you two were sworn enemies."

Simone inhaled through her nose, then blew out the breath. "Mariah changed. People do, Carl."

Carl raised his hands in surrender. "My bad."

"Let's go sit and enjoy some music, okay?" Simone

wished she'd said no to this disaster of a first date. She'd have been happier staying home and watching a rom-com or a Biggest Loser rerun on TV.

~

Gabe's heart jumped when he spied Simone being dragged by the hand toward their little group. Was this the tool she was engaged to? He looked the guy up and down. He already disliked him. The frown on Simone's face said she wasn't super happy to be at the concert.

It looked like they were having an argument after Simone's friend, Mariah arrived. Too bad he couldn't read lips.

"I remember you from high school," Mariah said, shaking Gabe's hand. "What a great athlete you were. Do you still play ball?"

Gabe shook his head. "Going pro was never an option. I couldn't make the cut, so I went in a different direction."

"That's too bad," Mariah said. "Your Senior year I went to every baseball game. Well, anyway, welcome back to Main."

"I'm not really 'back'," Gabe said. "I'm only here for a month, helping my dad out."

Before Mariah could respond, her fiancé pulled her away to greet some teenagers. "Talk later," she said with a wave of her fingers.

Simone and her guy rejoined them. Simone had her arms crossed and looked furious. Her fiancé waved toward a guy in a police uniform and moved away to talk with him.

Gabe sat on a chair and tapped the empty chair next to him. She glanced at him, then at Carl, and back at him.

"I promise not to bite," Gabe said with a grin.

Simone sank onto the chair. Her friend Mariah sat next to her, leaving Carl searching for an empty seat as the performers took the stage.

"Thanks," Simone whispered.

"Looks like your fiancé needs a seat," Gabe said, tilting his head toward Carl.

"Fiancé?" Simone said. The rest of her words were drowned out by the sudden blast of guitar through the massive outdoor speakers.

Gabe settled back to listen to some country rock, determined to enjoy beating out Carl the Tool for a seat with Simone.

The first band was a local group, meant to warm up the crowd and gather the latecomers. Their thirty-minute set included some classic country tunes that had everyone singing along. Gabe leaned toward Simone and said, "They're pretty good."

She nodded but didn't respond. He'd have to up his game. Why he wanted Simone's attention was a mystery to himself. But there it was.

He practically had to shout in Simone's ear to be heard. "What's your favorite kind of music?"

Simone leveled her gaze at him. Gabe hadn't realized her eyes were an unusual shade of green with flecks of brown. He studied her face, captivated by her natural beauty. She didn't wear a speck of makeup that he could tell. His gaze dropped to her lips when she ran her tongue over them. His breath hitched as he wondered what it would be like to kiss her.

She blinked and turned her gaze away, breaking the spell.

Chapter 10

Simone wanted to go home. Carl kept turning around in his seat to glare at Gabe and Mariah, who sat on either side of her. Gabe didn't get the hint that Carl was her date. Instead he kept trying to talk over the music, which was super annoying.

Also annoying was the fact that he had a great singing voice. And he wasn't embarrassed to belt out the songs with the band.

And what was the deal with him asking about her fiancé? Did he really think she and Carl were . . .

Ugh. Maybe she could feign sickness or a sudden migraine so Carl would have to take her home.

The first group finished their set and everyone stood to stretch. Carl scooted around the people standing nearby to shoulder his way to her side.

"Want something to drink?"

"Sure. Diet anything," Simone responded.

Carl sent a glare in Gabe's direction before heading toward the line of people at the concession stand.

Gabe nodded his head toward Carl's back. "What's with the hostility?"

The last thing Simone wanted was to get into a conversation with Glory Hog. "Not everyone is going to bow down and kiss your feet." Simone uttered the words, then wished she could take them back. "I'm sorry. That was rude."

Gabe leaned back and guffawed. "But honest." He shoved his hands in the pockets of his shorts. "What torture do you have planned for me this week?"

Simone glanced down at his bare legs. He wore a pair of golf shorts. Dang those legs. Simone felt herself grow hot as her eyes traveled up to Gabe's smirking lips.

"You'll have to wait until Monday." The workout she'd planned would likely kill him. Or at least take some of his cockiness down a notch.

Simone looked over to see Carl nearing the front of the drink line. What she really wanted was an ice cream cone. Fluffy's Ice Cream always had a mobile stand at the concerts.

As if he could read her mind, Gabe said, "Come with me. I'm going to get an ice cream cone. You look like you could use one too."

Simone swung her gaze to Carl. "Okay."

She followed Gabe out of the venue and down the street to where the Fluffy's had set up their truck. The line was mercifully short.

"Are you familiar with the band that's up next?" Gabe asked.

"Yeah, they come every year. They do mostly classic rock. Some country. They appeal to the older crowd. But they're good."

"I miss these concerts," Gabe said with a wistful sigh. "I'm usually busy working that I don't hear about stuff like this happening in Portland."

They ordered double scoop cones and sauntered

back toward the venue. "Thanks for this," Simone said. "There's nothing like Fluffy's on a summer night."

Gabe raised his cone in a mock salute. "Amen to that."

When they reached the area where the chairs were, Carl approached them with a scowl.

"Where'd you disappear off to? The ice is all melted in your drink."

Gabe spoke first. "Sorry, man. Your lady here looked like she needed some comfort food."

Simone almost felt sorry for Carl. But the feeling of cold ice cream sliding down her throat smothered her sympathy.

"Let's find a seat, Simone. Together." Carl sent one more glare toward Gabe before taking Simone's arm and pulling her to two empty seats.

Once they were seated, Carl leaned toward her. "I came back and you were gone. You could have at least waited for me." He sounded petulant.

"Sorry," Simone said. *Not sorry.*

Her eyes followed Gabe as he chatted with some of their old high school friends and a few others she didn't recognize. He seemed at ease with everyone, slapping backs and giving fist bumps. They were probably telling him what a great guy he was, saving the life of the motorcyclist.

Simone turned her gaze back to her date. "Have you ever had Fluffy's Ice Cream?" She asked.

"Heck no. I don't eat sweets."

Simone's stomach sank. Why work out if you couldn't enjoy some frozen heaven on a cone? On a scale of one to ten, this date hovered around a one. Her attention was caught once again when she heard Gabe's hearty laughter. He was using the rest of his ice cream cone like a baseball bat, swinging it around as he spoke to his friends. Yes, he had a little extra weight around his waist, but that would be gone by the time she finished with him. He was still pretty darn cute in his golf shorts and black tee shirt.

"What are you looking at?" Carl said in her ear as the next band took the stage.

"Nothing." Simone crunched down on her cone, determined to try to salvage the rest of the date. It was a beautiful summer evening in Main. The smell of fried food mixed with ocean air blowing off the coast was the best part of summer.

That and good music. Despite having a date who didn't eat sweets and being in the same air space with Glory Hog.

When the last note of the final song faded into the dusk, Simone was more than ready to head home.

"Want to get something to eat?" Carl asked.

Simone faked a yawn. "No, I'm kinda tired. I had a lot of clients today." Including one who hovered nearby.

Carl led her back to his car. "I have to work tomorrow, but I'm off Sunday. Want to do something?"

This was the worst part of dating. Having to decide after the first date if there would be a second. If not, how to gracefully decline.

"I can't," Simone answered. "I drive into Salem every Sunday and go to church with my parents."

"What about after church." The guy was nothing if not persistent.

"I go to their house for lunch and hang out with my sister. When I get back into Main, I have a standing date with my friends on Sunday night.”

“Your friend Lizzy?”

Simone nodded. “Yes. And Mariah.”

Carl shook his head. “I still don’t get it. You guys hated each other in school.”

Simone fiddled with her promise ring. “Do you go to church, Carl?”

“Once in a while. Why?”

Simone chose her words carefully, trying to avoid ‘Christian-ese.’ “Mariah had what you might call a come to Jesus meeting. She’s different. Still blunt, but softer.”

Carl was silent for a few beats. “Whatever.”

Simone bristled at his flippant response. This first date would also be the last. By the time Carl dropped her off at her apartment, the headache she planned to fake became too real.

“Don’t worry about walking me to my door,” Simone said before Carl could unfasten his seatbelt. “I have a raging headache.” She climbed out of the car and strode to her apartment door without glancing back.

What a jerk.

~

Gabe watched Simone practically dragged away from the concert by her fiancé. What a tool. What did Simone see in him? He’d tried to enjoy the second band, but his gaze kept returning to Simone and that guy. Her body language spoke volumes.

Gabe had gotten a shaft of pleasure over ticking the guy off when they’d come back with ice cream. He’d looked seriously bent.

He’d had fun reconnecting with old friends. It seemed like everyone heard about the accident and his role in saving the guy's life. Someone mentioned the City Council might want to give him an award. Gabe hoped it was a rumor. He didn't need that kind of attention.

When Gabe arrived home, his sister was still awake and lying in their dad's recliner.

"Hi. How was the concert?" Grace asked.

Gabe sank onto the sofa and laid his head back. "It was good. Both bands were good."

"Who all was there?"

Gabe shrugged. "A few people from high school."

"Come on, little brother, please give me some details. I've been stuck here for days, and I'm so bored I could cry."

"What's it worth to you?" Gabe asked, squinting at his sister.

Grace appeared to consider her answer. "I'll let you win next time we play cribbage."

Gabe shook his head. "Not good enough."

Grace adjusted the recliner to more of a sitting position. "Gabriel Bruce Harrison, you talk to me right now or I'm telling Mom."

Gabe raised both hands in surrender with a chuckle. "Fine." He rubbed his chin with one hand. "Let's see. There was Vivian Brown, I think she was the year between you and me. She's Vivian Anderson now. Her husband isn't from here."

"Go on."

"There was a bunch of people from my class. Robbie, Carson, Suzanna. A few others."

"I remember them. Who else?"

"The rest you probably don't know. They graduated after me. You'd already gone on to college."

"Was your personal trainer there?"

Gabe closed his eyes, remembering how Simone had taken her ice cream cone from his hand. Her long fingers wrapped around the cone as she energetically licked the drips of ice cream on the sides. How he'd wanted to kiss the ice cream off her lips to see what she tasted like.

"Gabe? You still awake?" Grace's voice penetrated his wandering thoughts.

"Uh, yeah. She was there. With her fiancé, Carl."

"I thought her fiancé's name was Adam."

Gabe scratched his ear. "I'm pretty sure his name is Carl. Someone called him Monty, though, so I could be wrong."

Grace stifled a yawn. "On that note, I better get to bed. If Mom finds me out here, she'll pitch a fit. She's worse than she ever was when we were kids."

Gabe watched his sister struggle to her feet. "Need some help, Sis?"

Grace rested her hands on her swollen belly. "No, I'm okay. I get a little winded sometimes. Sleep well."

But he didn't sleep well. Why did he keep thinking about Simone, engaged to that tool? Why did it matter, anyway? She was spoken for and he'd be gone in a little less than a month.

Still, he couldn't get his mind off the way her hair swung around her face. And how she looked in her running tights.

Stop, he told himself again. Not only is she out of your league, she's also out of touch.

But at least he had Monday to look forward to. Another workout and another chance to get to know her better.

Chapter 11

Sunday morning dawned cloudy with a hint of rain. Simone slid her bedroom window closed, shutting out the coastal fog and impending drizzle. When her folks lived in Main, Dad always said, if you don't like the weather, wait ten minutes.

She pulled on one of her two dresses and gathered her hair into a clip at the back of her neck. The thirty-minute drive to her parents' church would give her a chance to wake up. After a side trip to The Human Bean for a large mocha.

Her phone on the bathroom counter buzzed with a text.

Mariah: Your new client is Gabe Harrison????

Simone grimaced. She and Mariah hadn't been able to talk at the concert the night before. She sent a thumbs up emoji, hoping it would fend off any more comments. Didn't work.

Mariah: Holy cats! He's hot!

Simone: He's a pain in my backside. His ego is too big for Main.

Simone shoved the phone in her purse, ignoring the buzz from Mariah's response. Time to get some liquid caffeine and head to church.

After church, she hoped her parents would have more news on their plans. If they were serious about moving to California, Simone might consider going with. Anything would be better than staying here.

She'd never been anywhere except in her home state of Oregon. What would it be like to go somewhere else? She longed to travel and explore, even if only in the US. She and Adam had plans to take an extended honeymoon doing the Camino De Santiago hike in Spain. It would take them a little over a month to complete the journey. That dream crashed and burned in the wake of Adam's departure.

After church, Simone drove to her parents' house.

"Hi, darling." Simone's mother's greeting was accompanied by a kiss on her cheek. "I made your favorite lunch today."

"Spinach salad?" Simone asked.

"Of course. With a nice, broiled chicken breast cut up on top."

"Yummy. Where's Olivia? I didn't see her in church."

Her mom's face fell. "She wasn't feeling good this morning. I told her to stay home."

Simone lowered her voice. "How's she doing, really?"

Her mom held her hand out and shifted it from side to side. "So so. Depends on the day."

Since her sister's diagnosis of Multiple Sclerosis, her parents' every waking moment was spent on helping Olivia cope with the debilitating effects of the disease. And searching for expert answers for treatment. So far, they'd only been able to treat the disease, not cure it.

Mom patted Simone's hand. "We'll talk more over lunch. Your dad should be home any minute."

Simone was used to her father dawdling at church. She and Olivia and their mom had learned long ago to take separate cars to church. As a church Bishop, Dad often stayed behind to meet with parishioners or visitors to their church.

"Hey, Sis."

Simone turned when she heard Olivia's soft voice behind her. Simone moved to pull her sister into a hug. Simone felt her sister's shoulder bones poking through her blouse, evidence of more weight loss. Mom had said Olivia was depressed since learning there was no cure for MS.

Simone forced herself to smile at her younger sister. "What's this I hear about you missing church? I never got to stay home. Dad would have forcefully removed me from the bed if I'd try to get out of worship."

Olivia sent her a ghost of a smile. "Guess that's one of the advantages of being the youngest." She sank onto a kitchen chair as if a fifty-pound weight rested on her back.

Simone and her mom exchanged a worried glance.

"I'll get the salads out of the refrigerator. Simone, will you please set the table?"

Their dad arrived home full of good cheer from his morning at church. "How are all my beautiful girls this afternoon?" He gave each of them a kiss on the cheek. "What's for lunch, Mama? I'm starving."

Dad gave a moving prayer of thanks for the meal, and they all tucked into the food. Simone watched Olivia push the spinach around on her plate, only taking a bite or two.

"What's the latest on the potential move to California?" Simone asked.

Dad set his fork down and wiped his mouth with a napkin. "I'm glad you asked. Stanford Medicine has a clinical trial for people with Olivia's condition. We've applied and we're waiting for acceptance."

Simone almost smiled at her dad's reluctance to call Olivia's disease by name. Dad felt that to name it would make it somehow more real than it already was.

Mom set her fork down too. "We're looking at the Atherton, California or Campbell locations. Both are in the San Francisco area."

Simone let that information sink in. Was she brave enough to start over in a big city like San Francisco? She'd heard reports of crime and homelessness running rampant in the Bay Area. Maybe the two towns Mom mentioned wouldn't be as bad. She'd do an internet search when she got home.

"When do you think you'll hear back from them?" Simone asked.

Mom looked at Dad and shrugged. Olivia had remained quiet during their conversation. Her head stayed down and she seemed focused on her plate.

Simone nudged Olivia with her shoulder. "I think it sounds exciting. Going someplace new, meeting new people. What do you think Olivia?"

Olivia raised her shoulders and let them drop. "I guess."

Simone sighed. What could she do to bring a smile to her sister's face? In the meantime, it was time to hustle back to Main for the highlight of her week—coffee with her besties.

~

Gabe got dressed for church at his mother's insistence. He'd gotten out of the habit of church attendance since leaving home. His faith was still intact, though a bit dormant from lack of use.

Pastor Roy greeted him at the door like an old friend. "Heard you had some excitement last week."

Gabe shrugged, trying to maintain nonchalance. "Yeah, I guess."

"You're a hero, young man. Own it."

Before Gabe could respond, someone called for the pastor's attention.

The church had grown since he'd left. Gabe nodded to Mariah's fiancé, Ethan, sitting among a group of teenagers.

Gabe glanced around, hoping to see Simone. Disappointed, he settled into his seat next to his parents. He promised Grace a full report of who he talked to when he got back to the house. Poor Grace. Her sanguine personality craved social interaction. He'd ask Mom if it would be okay to invite some old friends over to hang out. Maybe watch a movie or something. He could invite his personal trainer too and maybe watch a sports flick.

Church was over and Gabe hadn't heard more than a couple of words Pastor Roy preached. *Sorry, God.*

Gabe took one more look around in case he'd missed Simone's entrance. At least that fiancé of hers wasn't there. He'd like to smack the guy upside the head.

Sorry, God. Again.

"Are we working today, Dad?" Gabe asked as they headed for his dad's Suburban.

"Sunday is a day of rest. I'm planning to go home,

have lunch, and take a nap."

Gabe grinned at his dad. "That sounds like a great plan. For you."

"What are you going to do this afternoon?" His mom asked.

Gabe feigned nonchalance. "I think I'll head over to Gym Time and get in a quick workout." And maybe catch a glimpse of the lovely Simone.

But first, to give Grace a full report of church. Maybe she wouldn't ask about the sermon. A guy could hope, right?

~

Simone spied her friends at their usual table at Cookie's Café.

"How was your date?" Lizzy didn't wait for Simone to get seated before asking the question.

"Yeah," Mariah said. "It didn't look like you had a great time with Monty, I mean Carl."

Simone dropped her purse on her lap. "It could have been better."

"Details, girlfriend, details," Lizzy insisted.

"Wait," Mariah interrupted. "Gabriel Harrison? Your new client?" Mariah leaned forward and tapped the table. "Spill, girlfriend."

Simone's blood pressure shot up. Not him again. Could they talk about something else? Please? She raised her eyes to the ceiling.

Lizzy's glance slid from Mariah to Simone. "What's going on?"

Mariah leaned forward. "Gabriel Harrison was at the concert Friday night." She glanced sideways at Simone. "He bought our friend here an ice cream cone. Anyway, Ethan told me the City Council wants to give him some kind of award for saving that guy's life. The one who had the motorcycle accident."

Lizzy held out a hand. "Wait." She pointed at Simone. "Your Glory Hog is Gabe Harrison?"

Simone's mouth turned down. "Yup."

Lizzy sank back against her chair. "Wow."

"It gets better. He's my new client."

"What?"

Simone shrugged.

Mariah tapped a long, red-tipped fingernail on the table. "Does anyone else know you got there first?"

Simone shrugged again.

"Someone needs to know," Mariah insisted.

Simone could practically hear the wheels turning in Mariah's head. "Don't bother. It really doesn't matter. Let him have his fifteen minutes of fame. He's going back to Portland at the end of the month." Her indifferent words were a sharp contrast to the heat building inside at the unfairness of life.

Speaking of unfair, Simone still hadn't had the chance to tell her friends about her parent's potential move to California. Time to change the subject.

"How are you feeling?" Simone asked Lizzy.

"Fat and ugly." Lizzy rubbed her tummy with a grim smile. "This one seems like he's growing a lot faster than Abby did."

"Maybe it's two," Mariah commented.

"Don't say that! One is enough, thank you very much. Besides, the doctor only sees one. I can't even imagine what it would be like to have twins." Lizzy shuddered.

"Speaking of twins, did you know Gabe's sister is on complete bed rest? His mom is watching Grace's twins." Mariah sat back with a smirk.

Lizzy laughed. "Aren't you the little gossip girl?"

Mariah sniffed. "It isn't gossip. It's news."

Lizzy laughed again. "You keep telling yourself that, friend."

"I can't help it if Ethan gets all the news from people in the church. Those teenagers are like a high school locker room. They tell him all the good stuff."

"How are you liking being engaged to a youth pastor?" Simone asked. Two years ago, if anyone had said Mariah would get married to a pastor, she would have laughed in their face.

Mariah placed her hand over her heart with a sappy smile. "It's amazing. Ethan is amazing. Youth work is—"

"Amazing!" Lizzy and Simone said at the same time. They dissolved into giggles.

Simone had no desire to change the mood by talking about her family drama, so she buried it under 'to be discussed next time.'

"Well, ladies, I better get home. I have an early day tomorrow and some sweet revenge to plan for Glory Hog's workout."

She stood and scooted out the door before Lizzy or Mariah could respond. They'd no doubt want details which she wasn't ready to divulge.

Chapter 12

Gabe took a deep breath before pushing open the door to Gym Time. The good part of this afternoon would be spending time with the beautiful and sometimes charming Simone. The bad part would also be spending time getting his butt kicked by Simone.

Simone waited for him in Carson's office.

"Ready?" she asked, waving goodbye to Carson.

"What are we doing today?" Gabe asked, hustling to catch up to her.

Simone glanced over her shoulder with a wicked smile. "You'll see."

She headed out of the gym and toward her very orange colored Honda. "Hop in," she said as the key fob chirped.

"Where we going?" Gabe climbed in and fastened his seat belt.

"You'll see," Simone repeated.

Simone pointed the car down Uglow Street. Gabe wracked his brain for something to talk about as they traveled the rolling hills outside of Main.

"Great concert Friday night," he said.

"It was okay."

"Did your fiancé like it too?"

Simone shot him a glare. "Fiancé?"

"Yeah. Carl what's-his-name."

Simone started laughing so hard she had to gasp for breath.

"What did I say?" Gabe asked, scratching his head.

"Carl Montgomery is not my fiancé."

Gabe let his hand drop into his lap. "If you're not engaged to him, then why were you on a date with him?" What was with this woman? Was she one of those females who couldn't go anywhere without a man? He'd have a fit if his fiancée stepped out with another guy.

Simone seemed to struggle to maintain her composure. "I'm trying to figure out what business this is of yours. My dating life is not your concern."

"No need to get all snippy." Gabe crossed his arms over his chest. "It seems like," he drew out the words, "if you're engaged to one guy, you don't usually date another."

Simone kept her eyes facing the windshield. "Carl and I go way back to high school. He asked me out. I said yes. End of story."

Gabe let her words settle into his spirit. His heart did a quick upbeat as he considered what that meant. It meant, dummy, that even if she was engaged, she went out with other guys. As friends, maybe? He hid his smile behind a fake yawn.

A few minutes later, Simone pulled into the parking area for Basket Slough.

"I haven't been here for years," Gabe said, climbing out of the car and inhaling. The grass had turned brown, but the recent rain brought up a damp hay smell. "My buddies and I used to come up here on Friday and

Saturday nights and drink beer."

Simone sent him a disapproving glare. "Figures."

"Are we gonna hike the Morgan Lake Trail?" Morgan Trail was a little over three miles and was a nice uphill climb followed by downhill. The trail wound around trees and scrub, often flushing out deer and other wildlife.

"No, we're not going to hike it. We're going to run." Simone reached into the backseat of her car and pulled out a backpack, handing it to him.

Gabe tested its weight. "Sheesh, Simone. What's in this?"

Simone grinned. "Fifty-pound weights. Put it on and let's get started."

~

Simone experienced a twinge of amusement watching Gabe's face as he slipped on the backpack. He struggled to settle the pack comfortably over his shoulders. She took only a moment to admire his muscular calves before starting up the first hill with a slow jog.

Halfway up the hill, Simone turned around to see Gabe standing at the bottom of the hill. Jogging back down, she stopped and put her hands on her hips.

"What's the problem?

"You want me to run this course carrying fifty pounds?"

"That is correct." Simone cocked her head. "Next time the pack will be heavier."

"Understood."

"Then let's get with it. Oh, by the way, we're going to do two laps. A little over six miles."

Before she could start up the hill again, Gabe

stopped her.

"Wait. I have a proposition for you."

Simone pressed her lips together and waited. What did Glory have in mind? By the sly look on his face, it couldn't be good.

Gabe rubbed the stubble on his chin. "If I can make the first lap around the Slough without stopping, will you agree to go out with me?"

Simone's mouth dropped open. Was he serious? It was hard to tell from the goofy grin on his face.

She placed her hands on her hips. "Look, Glory, my job is to train you to make it up a hundred and ten flights of stairs without dying." Simone waved a hand around the landscape. "That's what we're doing here."

"Right on. But I like a little competition to make things interesting. What do you say? One lap without stopping and you go to next Friday night's concert. With me. As friends."

Simone stared at Gabe without blinking. Her brain whirled at a hundred miles an hour. After a dating drought for the past several months, now she had two guys ask her out within a week?

She didn't give herself a chance to think. "Two laps without stopping."

Gabe's eyebrows shot up. "Two?"

Simone grinned. "To make it interesting. You did say you like competition."

Gabe seemed to consider her words. He shifted the backpack up, holding onto the straps. "Okay."

"Okay?" Simone's smile faded. This guy was serious. She shrugged. "Okay, big guy, let's see what you're made of."

~

Gabe couldn't believe Simone had agreed to his spontaneous plan. He hadn't intended to ask her out right then, but the words flew from his mouth on their own. The fact that she'd doubled-down cracked him up. The problem was, he was confident he could make the first lap, even with the extra weight strapped on his back. But two laps? Doubtful.

He'd have plenty of time to think up a Plan B. Six miles of time.

The first incline increased his heart rate. A quick check of his smart watch showed he hadn't reached peak heart rate yet. The trail wound through the trees, letting in dappled sunlight. Until the sweat began to drip into his eyes, Gabe had a great view of Simone's backside as she set the pace in front of him.

As soon as he could get enough air in his lungs to breath, he'd ask her about the ring she wore. Where was her fiancé? He smiled to remember how she'd barely been able to stop laughing in the car when he thought she was engaged to that Carl guy.

Relief caused him to increase his pace, before regretting it. Gabe's breath came in gasps. Simone glanced over her shoulder with a concerned look.

"You okay?" she asked.

Gabe waved a hand. "Fine," he gasped.

By the time the trail dropped back toward the parking lot, Gabe was ready to die. He'd be the one receiving CPR from Simone.

He glanced up the first hill with a groan.

"We can rest if you want," Simone said.

"No. Keep." *Gasp.* "Going." Gabe jogged up the hill with Simone on his heels. He hated her at that moment. She seemed barely winded, while he struggled to catch even a gasp of air.

At the top, Gabe gave up the pretense of being able to make the two laps. He leaned over, resting his hands on his thighs. Sweat dripped from his face, wetting the dirt.

He turned his head to look at Simone, expecting a triumphant grin. Instead, her face scrunched with concern.

Simone grabbed his wrist and pulled his watch toward her to read his heart rate.

"Let's walk around up here." She pulled him toward the lookout area. "Don't stop completely or lactic acid will build up in your muscles."

Simone helped him remove the pack. Dropping it on one of the wooden benches, she pushed him toward the fence. "Take a couple of laps up here before we start down."

Gabe felt his heart rate slow and his breathing increase. After a few laps around the small lookout point, Simone pointed him in the direction back down the first hill.

"Let's walk to the bottom." She picked up the backpack and slung it over one shoulder.

"Want me to carry that?"

Simone shook her head with a frown. "I've got it."

At the bottom of the hill, Simone unlocked her car and retrieved two bottles of water from a small cooler on the floor of the back seat.

Gabe took the water and downed half of it. He used the tail of his shirt to dry his face.

Simone sipped on her water with a faraway look on her face. "I'm sorry." She cast a quick glance in Gabe's direction before looking away.

"Sorry?" What did she have to be sorry about?

"I shouldn't have pushed you that hard."

Gabe laid a hand on her arm. "I'm to blame, not you. I shouldn't have thrown out that challenge."

The corners of Simone's mouth turned down. "No, it was stupid of me to double the bet. You're not ready."

Gabe increased the pressure on her arm. She looked so upset he wished he could pull her into his arms. But they were both a sweaty mess. Besides, he was pretty sure she'd shove him away and possibly smack him with the weighted backpack.

"Will you still go out with me?"

~

No doubt about it, the guy was bold. Simone couldn't believe she'd agreed to a date with Glory Hog. At least he'd be gone soon and there wouldn't be a second date.

She reminded herself of what she'd told her besties: The worst part of dating was going out on a date.

Simone showered and sank onto her couch while dinner warmed in the microwave. Mom had sent home leftovers, as per usual. She'd made a pot roast on Saturday and had kept some aside for Simone to take home. The spinach salad they'd had on Sunday had been completely devoured. Except for her sister's uneaten food. Another worry along with the one Simone carried from today's workout with Gabe.

She still berated herself over the dumb challenge she'd given him. They'd only run five miles twice in the past week. To expect him to be able to carry extra weight and jog over six miles was incredibly stupid. No wonder she was still in Main, working as a personal trainer to a bunch of geriatric men and women and bridezillas wanting to lose weight fast.

Not that she didn't love her clients and the regulars at the gym. She thought of Bob, who came five days a week to work on the stair climb machine. Roger loved the elliptical and his wife, Sue used the small indoor pool to swim laps.

The microwave dinged. Simone got to her feet and shuffled into the kitchen. If only her life was different. She felt a twinge of envy for her parents. They got to plan a move to a new place. They'd get to explore their new state and make new friends. Once Olivia's condition stabilized, they'd probably travel again.

Meanwhile, Simone was stuck here in Main.

She ate her dinner in front of the television. Her doorbell rang as she took the last bite. She hoped it was the Amazon delivery guy. He always flirted a little when he dropped off her packages. He had great legs, too.

Which pulled her thoughts back to Glory Hog with the great legs. It wasn't fair for a guy to have legs better shaped than hers.

Simone flung upon the door with a smile on her face. It faded when it was Gabe standing on her doorstep.

"What are you doing here?"

Chapter 13

Gabe expected a warmer greeting than "What are you doing here?"

"I, uh, wanted to make sure where you lived so I could, you know, pick you up Friday."

Simone's eyes narrowed as she regarded him. "Okay."

Gabe felt like a bug under a microscope. What was it about this woman that made his tongue lose all connection to his brain? "Okay. So."

What else could he say? He'd stopped her on a whim after picking up some materials from the feed store for his dad. Carson had given Gabe Simone's address, along with a ration of teasing.

"Good luck," Carson had said. "The woman is untouchable. You know she's engaged, right?"

Gabe had quickly told his buddy that Simone was not, repeat, not engaged.

Carson's laugh had been deep and long. "She's engaged to God, dude. She won't date anyone who isn't a Christian. You'd better sharpen your faith, friend, if you want a chance with her."

During the short drive to her apartment, Gabe questioned his decision to ask Simone out. Now that he was at her door, he wondered at the wisdom of going out with someone religious. Especially after his fall from grace with Tiffany.

He was here now. He opted for humor to break the frigid air emanating from Simone. "I'm just a guy, standing in front of a girl, asking her to let him into her apartment." He pasted a grin on his face, giving her his best puppy-dog eyes.

Simone pursed her lips, then swung open the door. "Come on in. I can't have the neighbors thinking I'm heartless."

Gabe's smile became genuine. "Thanks." He looked around at her spare furnishings. A small flat-screen TV was mounted on one wall. On a bookshelf underneath sat photos of her with two women, one he remembered from the concert. Mariah. He didn't recognize the other. Another framed photo sat face down on the bookshelf.

"Would you like something to drink?" Simone asked.

"Sure. Anything."

When Simone disappeared into the kitchen, Gabe took hold of the frame to peek at the hidden picture. It was Simone in what looked like a cocktail dress with a dark-haired guy wearing a suit. He had his hand around her shoulders, while hers rested on his chest. They gazed at each other with obvious adoration. Embarrassed, he set the photo down. Who was the guy?

Simone returned to the living room with two sports drinks. "Which one, lemon-lime or grape."

"Tough choice," Gabe said, pretending to consider each one. He watched Simone's body language to determine which one she preferred. "I'll take the grape one."

Nailed it, it told himself. She looked relieved at his choice.

"Have a seat." Simone motioned toward the sofa. She sat on a side chair and tucked one leg underneath her.

Gabe cracked open the drink and took a sip.

Simone did the same. "I really hope you're not mad about today," she said. "That was really dumb of me—"

"Stop. I'm fine. I'm the one who should apologize." He shrugged. "I couldn't think of another way to get you to go out with me." He dropped his gaze to his lap.

"You could have asked."

Gabe picked at the label with his thumb. "Would you have said yes?"

"Probably not."

Gabe grinned over at her. "I've gotta be an improvement over your last date."

Simone smile spread wide and she laughed. "Carl the cop." She shook her head. "Yeah, that was a mistake."

"On a scale of one to ten, was he a two or a one?"

Simone tapped her lips with one finger. "I'm gonna say a one," she said, playing along.

"After Friday, you let me know where I fall on that scale, okay?"

Simone grinned. "I can already give you a score."

Gabe raised his eyebrows. "Really?"

"Well, yeah. You bought me ice cream. You're a solid five."

Gabe pretended to pout. "Only a five? I'm going to have to see how I can improve my score."

Simone shrugged. "You have four days to work on your game."

Gabe grinned back at her. What a breath of fresh air this woman was.

Simone's question hit him from left field. "Why are you really here?"

~

Simone hadn't intended to be that blunt. Her friend Mariah was rubbing off on her. But she needed to know why this guy was determined to date her. Especially since he was headed back to who-knew-where at the end of the month.

Gabe's forehead wrinkled. "Why am I here? I told you. I wanted to be sure I had the right address before Friday."

Simone stared into his blue eyes, gauging his honesty. "Why me? There are a dozen women in this city who'd go out with you like that." She snapped her fingers.

Gabe crossed one leg over the other knee. "You like ice cream."

Simone huffed out a laugh. "That's your criteria for dating? Ice cream?"

Gabe shrugged. "I'm a simple man."

Simone considered his answer before changing the subject. "The City Council plans to honor you later this month at their meeting." The news of the announcement still rankled.

Gabe's face grew pink. "I know. I'm trying to figure out how to get out of it."

"Maybe you should tell them who really saved the guy's life."

Gabe laughed. "Let's do a little memory jogging, shall we? I arrived at the scene to find you pumping the guy's chest while desperately trying to figure out how to get back to your car to get your cell phone.”

He paused long enough for Simone to suck in a breath. What nerve!

“I arrived and took over CPR so you could use my phone to call 9-1-1. If I hadn’t gotten there, the guy would have died before you got to your car and back.”

“You don’t know that.”

“How long were you doing CPR before I got there?”

Simone pinched her lips together. She wouldn’t give him the satisfaction of answering.

Gabe spread his hands. “See? Exactly like I thought.”

Simone shot to her feet. “You should go.”

Gabe sent her a lazy grin. “The truth hurts, doesn’t it?” He took his time gathering his legs under him and getting to his feet.

“See you Wednesday,” he said as he headed out the door.

~

Gabe smiled to himself all the way to his truck. Simone was a lot like his sister. Feisty, blunt, and unwilling to back down. To say he was intrigued would be an understatement. Wednesday’s workout should be interesting.

In the meantime, his dad waited at home for the stuff Gabe picked up from the feed store.

At his parents’ house, the twins latched themselves onto him, begging him to play with them.

“Let’s go outside and get out of Grandma’s hair,” Gabe said. Mom sent him a grateful look. Chasing after twin four-year-olds had her looking haggard.

“Will you jump on the trampoline with us, Uncle

Gabe?" Mercy asked.

Gabe's legs still felt like cooked noodles, but he gave into the girls' begging and climbed onto the trampoline with them. Thirty minutes later, he begged to get off, leaving them bouncing as if they had more energy than the power company.

He sat in a lounge chair, watching the girls and thinking about Simone.

A few minutes later, Grace waddled out and sank onto the lounger next to him.

"Thanks for doing this, Gabe. I feel bad Mom watches the girls all day while I lie in bed like a slug."

Gabe rubbed a weary hand across his face, imagining what his mom must be going through.

"It's no problem," he said, even though he'd rather be sleeping off the grueling workout Simone had put him through.

Grace shifted her position on the lounger with a wince. "How's the training going?"

"It's going."

Grace sent him the stink-eye. "I need details, remember?"

Before he could answer, the girls called to their mom.

"Watch me, Mommy."

"No, watch me."

"I'm watching," Grace said. "You are not off the hook, little brother. I want to know everything."

Gabe smiled. "Fine. Today we—"

"Who's we?"

"My trainer, Simone Coleman and I went to Basket Slough." Gabe described the trail and how he'd had to carry fifty pounds on his back. The only thing he left out was their challenge.

"You like her," Grace said.

Gabe twisted his head to look at his sister, but her eyes were trained on Mercy and Hope. "What? Why would you say that? I don't like her. She's a sadist out to kill me."

He saw the beginnings of a smile creep up Grace's cheek.

"Your tone of voice changes when you say her name."

"It does not."

Grace pulled her gaze away from her girls and faced him. "Admit it, Gabe. You have a crush on your personal trainer."

Chapter 14

Gabe plumped his pillow for the fifteenth time since dropping into bed.

A crush, his sister had said. It made him sound like a middle schooler, crushing on a cute girl.

Well, aren't you?

Gabe told himself to shut up. What was wrong with wanting to go out with a pretty woman? He'd had plenty of dates since Tiffany's abrupt departure. Sure, none of them had affected him like Simone. It wasn't like he was a novice at dating.

Carson's words came back to him as he flipped from his right side to his left.

"She only dates Christians."

Gabe was a Christian. Did it matter that he hadn't been to church in years? He'd made a profession of faith in youth group when he was seventeen. Surely that counted as being a Christian.

A sliver of guilt pierced his spirit. When was the last time he'd prayed?

Ugh. Too long ago. Well, anyway, he'd enjoy some time with the lovely Simone before heading back to Portland and finding another job.

Gabe woke Wednesday morning with a feeling of

anticipation. What torture would his personal trainer have for him today? He smiled as he sauntered into the kitchen for his first cup of coffee.

He grabbed a mug from the cupboard. "Good morning, Mom," he said, pouring a cup from the silver carafe.

"You're awfully chipper this morning, "Mom said.

Gabe took his first appreciative sip and leaned back against the counter, crossing his ankles. "It's a beautiful day. I get to work outside with my dad, and I have some delicious coffee brewed by my loving mother."

His mom rolled her eyes. "I don't know what's gotten into you. But I hope you still feel as chipper after Dad has you on the combine for four hours."

Gabe dropped a kiss on her cheek and headed to his bedroom to get dressed.

Later that day, he hopped into his truck and pointed it to Gym Time.

He found Simone in Carson's office, deep in discussion. He rapped twice on the door frame.

"Am I interrupting?" he asked.

"Not at all. Simone and I were going over your workout schedule."

Gabe clapped his hands together. "Great."

Carson pushed back from his desk. "I'm going to take you through your workout today."

Gabe swung his gaze from Carson to Simone, who kept her face averted. "Really? Why?"

"Simone has some things to do this afternoon. I'll be taking you through your paces."

Gabe swallowed his disappointment. It was obvious from Simone's body language that she wanted to avoid even looking at him.

"That's okay with you, right?" Carson asked.

"Uh, yeah. Fine. Let's go."

Simone looked up long enough to briefly make eye contact before pushing past him out the door. Something happened between yesterday and today. Gabe needed to investigate.

He followed Carson into the workout room. Carson had set it up like Simone had the week before, with five workout stations. Through the glass wall, he saw Simone climb into her bright orange car and pull out of the parking lot.

"Is she okay?" Gabe asked, inclining his head toward Simone's taillights.

"Who, Simone? Yeah, she's okay. She has a lot going on with her family. She hasn't been the same since she and her fiancé broke up."

Gabe filed this information away to think about later. Right now, he had to concentrate on getting back into shape. Otherwise, he'd never be able to prove he was able to complete the stair challenge.

The 9/11 stair challenge was a way for Gabe to stand in solidarity with his fallen brothers who made the ultimate sacrifice to save others. Which made his thoughts return to Simone. Why was she so bent over him getting recognized for saving the motorcyclist's life? He was the one who caused the guy to start breathing.

His conscience gave him a small twinge. Yes, she'd gotten there first. But still, he was the hero. Wasn't he?

~

Grateful for an understanding boss, Simone climbed in her car and headed toward the ocean. After her mom's phone call that morning, she needed some space. The coastal air and frigid water would help clear her head.

Simone pulled into a parking space at the beach access and grabbed a towel from the back seat of Orange Crush. Sand crunched under her feet on the asphalt before ending at the edge of the beach. The salty tang of the ocean breeze pulled her to the water's edge. She laid down her towel and dropped into a cross-legged position.

Her parents decided to move to North Dakota. Not California. Fargo, North Dakota to the Roger Maris Cancer Center.

Simone's little sister Olivia had cancer.

The diagnosis came out of left field, her dad had said. As a former baseball player, he used all the jargon. Her sister's MS had masked the symptoms of a brain tumor. Cassius had done hours of research since Monday and decided the remote cancer center in North Dakota would be the best place for Olivia to get treatment.

Pressure in Simone's chest pushed out the tears she'd been holding back since early that morning. The salt of her tears mixed with the salty air blowing from the water. Bowing her head, Simone let the tears fall.

What if Olivia died? Losing her had never been part of the equation. Her parents dealt with Olivia's diagnosis of Multiple Sclerosis the way they'd dealt with other challenges that had come their way. They'd sometimes faced blatant racism because of their marriage, but they'd faced the prejudice head-on with courage.

Hearing the fear in Mom's voice had undone her.

Simone swept the tears from her cheeks. She stood

and stripped down to her swimsuit, then approached the water, pulling her hair up into a rubber swim cap. The shock of fifty-eight-degree water on her ankles sent shivers up her legs. Simone continued to wade in before diving under a wave.

She came up sputtering before rising on an incoming wave. For ten minutes Simone battled through the water until her limbs grew numb with the cold. Heading for shore, she wrapped the towel around her shivering body.

Sitting down on the sand, she let the sun gradually warm her outside, even as her inside stayed cold.

How did someone face the loss of a sibling? How would her parents cope with Olivia's possible death?

Decisions needed to be made, but her brain felt as frigid as the Pacific Ocean. Decision like, should she go to North Dakota with her parents to help support them? Should she move back to Salem and stay in their home while they were gone? Would she now be free to take the vacation she always wanted, now that her parents wouldn't be in the same area code?

Simone raised her eyes to the clear sky overhead. *I need wisdom, Lord.*

The sun's rays grew hot the longer Simone sat. She prayed for Olivia, her parents, and wisdom for the doctors who would be evaluating and treating her sister.

Most of all she prayed for wisdom for herself. Gabe's face came to her mind and she pushed it away. She didn't have the bandwidth to deal with him. She'd allow herself one date, the Friday concert, and that would be that.

Simone dug into the pocket of her shorts lying on the sand when she heard it ring. She smiled when the caller ID showed her old college buddy, DavidJon McFarlane.

"Mr. DavidJon. What's up? I haven't talked to you in ages."

"Hey, girl. I'm calling to tell you about an opportunity."

"Hm. Sounds interesting, as long as you're not trying to talk me into a multi-level-marketing scheme."

DavidJon laughed. "Nope. This is way better. I'm opening a boutique gym up here in Beaverton and I wondered if you'd like to come work for me."

Simone grinned into the phone. "Would I have to call you Boss?"

"More like Supreme High Commander." He paused for a beat. "Seriously, Simone. You're the best trainer I've ever worked with. Why don't you come up next week and let me show you around. I've already got a location and all the equipment is on order. Please say yes."

Simone exhaled with a whoosh. "Wow, DJ. That's huge. Can I think about it and get back to you?"

"Oh, you bet, girl. I know you have to pray about it. I wouldn't want the Big Guy upstairs to get mad."

Simone shook her head. "The Big Guy upstairs has a name, you know."

"I know, I know. Yes, you think about it, pray about it, and do whatever it is you do. Then call me back and say yes."

"I will. And thanks, DavidJon."

Maybe this was exactly the thing she needed. A change of scene, a new job, and new opportunities. Simone did a quick search on the distance between Beaverton, Oregon and Fargo, North Dakota.

Ugh. Fifteen hundred miles. About the same as from Salem.

Simone stood and shook the sand off her clothes before slipping them back on. She trudged back to her car, got in, and cranked up the heater. Time to go back to her apartment and think about DavidJon's offer.

Chapter 15

Gabe returned to his parents' house sore and frustrated. He'd hoped to spend the two-hour workout with Simone but got Carson instead. It was like asking your mom for a piece of cake and she gives you a bowl of broccoli.

After a quick shower and a noisy dinner with his parents, Grace, and the twins, Gabe was ready to call it a night. He closed the door to his bedroom and stretched out on the bed, his back against the headboard. On every surface were reminders of his high school glory days. He missed the attention and the validation he was worth something. A smile worked its way up to his mouth. Simone's nickname held some merit.

The situation with Tiffany had been like getting nailed in the head by a wild pitch. That she'd casually rid herself of the baby they'd created grieved him still. A small part of him was relieved he wouldn't be chained to her for the rest of his life.

Did that make him a bad person? Probably. The Bible was full of warnings about being 'unequally yoked' to someone who didn't believe in God. Maybe he should have tried harder to bring Tiffany around to his Christian faith.

According to Carson, Simone was Miss Super Christian. She'd likely reject him in disgust when she learned of his history.

What difference did it make, anyway? In a few weeks, he'd head back to Portland. Or maybe to South Carolina.

Gabe pulled his phone near and opened the email app. He deleted several before seeing one from the Charleston South Carolina fire department. Nervous anticipation made his palms sweat as his finger hovered over the email. What would it be like to move across the country, away from his family? Gabe's goal had been to get as far away from Tiffany and their group of friends as he could. The job in Charleston was the perfect opportunity to escape. But at what cost?

What if his parents needed him again? Or Grace? Living in Portland was close enough to visit, but far enough away to have his life. Such as it was.

In his twenties, Gabe had expected to be married by this time with one or two kids. At thirty-two, those expectations were slowly crushed by reality.

Gabe took a deep breath and touched the screen to open the email.

~

Thursday came and went, and Simone still hadn't decided whether to explore DavidJon's offer. He'd sent her a couple of texts with days the following week for her to drive up to Beaverton to check out his new studio. She'd been vague in her responses.

During her quiet time that morning, Simone read and reread the Scripture verse of the day.

Joshua 1:9 "Have I not commanded you? Be strong

and of good courage; do not be afraid, nor be dismayed, for the Lord your God is with you wherever you go." (NKJV)

Simone knew in her heart that God would be with her, even if she moved to Beaverton, Oregon. Or if she moved to Fargo, North Dakota. But here in Main, she felt as if God's presence had departed. Why did her little sister have to suffer so much bad stuff in her young life? It didn't seem fair.

She remembered Dad's admonition from when she lived at home. Whenever she or her sisters complained that 'It isn't fair,' Dad would say, 'Life isn't fair. Get used to it.'

Dad had played college baseball. Several pro scouts had come to his games and Dad expected an offer from at least one of them. But a shattered ankle sliding into home base had destroyed that dream. Dad was the living, breathing, example of life's unfairness.

"Why Fargo, North Dakota?" Simone had asked when they'd talked on the phone yesterday.

Dad's answer brought a wave of doubt. "Roger Maris was Baseball's Single-Season Home Run King from 1961-1998. He hit sixty-one home runs during the 1961 season while he was a member of the New York Yankees. Maris also played for the Cleveland Indians, Kansas City Athletics, and St. Louis Cardinals."

"Yeah, but what does he know about cancer?"

"He passed away at age fifty-one, Simone. The center was founded in his name. It's his legacy."

Simone had swallowed the rest of her concerns. Once her dad's mind was made up, that was 'end of discussion.' She'd learned that lesson well during her childhood.

Thinking about her dad and his baseball career cut short brought her thoughts around to Gabe. He'd played baseball in high school and college. Did he also have a life-changing injury that kept him from going pro?

Why should she care? She had a job to do and that was to get him ready for a grueling stair climbing challenge. Once Simone was finished with their training, Gabe would scuttle back to Portland. They'd never likely cross paths again. Simone doubted she knew what Grace looked like.

If she looked anything like Gabe, she was probably gorgeous. Gabe had a Chris Pratt vibe going for him, but Gabe's eyes were blue. Simone pictured his nieces as blonde-haired blue-eyed cherubs. Growing up, Simone had envied girls with smooth, blond hair. She regularly flat-ironed the kinks out of her hair, preferring straight hair to the curls bestowed by her father. Eva and Olivia got their mom's hair. It was a source of irritation throughout her teen years. As an adult, Simone accepted as a fact of life that she was the perfect mixture of her parents' ethnicity.

A quick look at her smart watch had Simone scrambling to her feet. She dashed out the door and headed to work.

She breezed into Gym Time and headed into Carson's office to say hello.

"Thanks again for letting me go yesterday. How was the workout with Gabe?"

Carson's look was full of concern. "It went fine. More importantly, how are you?"

Simone shrugged. "As well as I can be. My folk's plan is to leave at the end of the month. They're flying up next week for an initial consultation, then move up once the doctors decide on a course of treatment."

Carson nodded, then stood and pulled Simone into a hug. "I'm sorry, Simone. This has got to be tough."

Simone let herself be comforted by her old friend. She'd miss this if she took DavidJon up on his offer. Carson knew everything about her life.

Carson pulled back and held Simone's upper arms. "Do you need to take some time off?"

Simone gave him a close-lipped smile. "No, I'll be better off working. It'll keep my mind off things." A sliver of guilt worked its way between her ribs. How could she consider leaving Carson and Gym Time? He'd been super easy to work with and to work for.

Why did the possibility of moving to Beaverton fill her with excitement?

~

Friday couldn't arrive fast enough. Gabe was so anxious to get to the gym and see Simone that it overshadowed the email he'd gotten from Charleston FD.

"We regret to inform you that the position has been filled."

There'd been more platitudes meant to placate the bluntness of the rejection, but it was apparent he wasn't even in the running for the job. It would have been a promotion from his current rank of driver engineer to lieutenant.

The only bright spot of the week was getting to know his personal trainer better. Unless she shuffled him off to Carson again.

His cell phone beeped with an incoming message as he pulled into the gym parking lot. He turned off the ignition and clicked on the message from his Captain.

Wills: When you get back, we need to talk

Gabe's stomach tightened. Was this a 'good talk' or a 'you'll soon be out of a job' talk? Captain Wills hadn't been excited over Gabe's leave of absence request. They'd been short-handed since the city had cut some of their budget. Gabe's absence left them with a hole in the battalion. To be blunt, Gabe's performance hadn't been stellar in the past few months. Hence, the extra pounds around his middle from too many beers with the boys on his days off. Too many fast-food meals and potato chips.

His text to Wills was short.

Okay.

Gabe waited for the bubbles to appear, showing Wills was responding, but the screen stayed static.

He tossed the phone into the glove box so it wouldn't weigh down his shorts during the workout. The phone dinged once more as Gabe snapped the glove box closed. Should he ignore it or see what his captain said.

Better to get it over with. He retrieved the phone and unlocked the screen. The text wasn't from Captain Wills but from Tiffany.

Tiffany: I miss you. Can we talk? Coffee or lunch?

This was followed by a smiley face with heart eyes.

Gabe snorted. Talk? That'd be the day. He owed his former girlfriend nothing. She'd disappeared out of his life and left him with smoldering ashes from their relationship.

He put the phone back in the glove box without responding.

Time to get back in shape. Physically, anyway.

Maybe hanging around Simone would be the impetus he needed to get his spiritual self back in shape too. Gabe pasted a smile on his face and headed into the gym.

He found Simone helping a middle-aged woman with the settings on one of the recumbent bikes.

The woman looked up at Simone with a rueful smile. "I never can figure out these settings. Thank you for your patience."

"Not a problem, Vicky. That's what I'm here for."

The woman reached out and tugged on Simone's arm. "They're lucky to have you here."

Simone's smile faded when she spied Gabe standing nearby.

"You're early," she commented.

Gabe's snappy response died at the worried lines around Simone's eyes. She looked like she hadn't slept well in a few days.

"Are you okay?" He reached out a hand.

Simone took a step back. "Fine. Are you ready for today?"

"Sure."

Simone indicated Gabe should follow her. She led him to the stair climbing machine. "I thought we'd see how you do on the stair climber." She leaned over to retrieve what looked like the same backpack he'd hefted on their run Monday.

She handed him the backpack as if it weighed less than a newborn baby. "According to my research, your gear weighs between forty-five and seventy-five pounds. Do you have any idea how much of your gear you'll be carrying on the challenge?"

"That sounds about right," Gabe answered. He took

the pack and shoved his arms through the straps. "How heavy is this?"

"Same as Monday. Fifty. I'm going to set the machine at a steady pace for thirty minutes. Does that sound okay?"

Gabe climbed on the machine with a quick nod. He could handle it for half an hour. "Are you gonna stay here in case I pass out?"

Simone huffed out a breath. "Come on, Glory Hog. Don't think you can handle a few stairs yet?"

Gabe grinned. "Oh, I can handle it okay. But how about you do it too?" He patted the machine next to him. "Let's both have a go, shall we?"

Simone glared at him. Gabe shrugged. "You can dish it out, but can you take it?" Why was he treating her like his sister? They'd challenged each other all through their growing up years. Physical challenges, mental challenges, anything and everything was a competition. What he really wanted to do was grab Simone and drag her down to the Human Bean and find out why her eyes looked red and puffy.

Simone stepped onto the stair machine next to him. "Fine, Glory. Let's see what ya got."

She set both their machines for thirty minutes with a five-minute warm up and the same for a cool down.

"Drive through your heels, not toes," Simone instructed. "Stand up tall and keep your spine neutral."

Gabe did as she instructed, feeling the heat building in his quads.

"Hold the handrails lightly in front of you," Simone said, taking hold of his hands and moving them into proper position.

Gabe's pulse sped up and his skin tingled from the

touch of her long brown fingers. He looked over to find her looking at him. "What?"

"Try to keep up, Glory."

"Challenge accepted." Gabe matched her pace and breathing and ignored the increasing tightness in his calves. He'd asked for this, he reminded himself. The memorial 9/11 challenge would give him a boost to his shredded self-confidence. He'd go back to Portland in better shape both physically and mentally. He'd have helped out his parents and hopefully watched his sister give birth to a healthy baby boy.

Gabe's eyes strayed to Simone's lithe form as she bounced on the machine. Although she was the same thin build as his former girlfriend, Tiffany couldn't hold a candle to Simone. Even without makeup and with sweat beginning to bead on Simone's forehead she was still prettier than Tiffany's overly made-up appearance. Simone's fingernails were cut short and without any color. Her dark hair hung straight to her chin.

His face burned when Simone caught him staring. "Sorry," Gabe muttered, turning his attention back to the timer. Ten minutes into the workout and his lungs felt like they would burst. Simone smiled and looked like she could climb stairs the rest of the day without a hitch. This was embarrassing.

Chapter 16

Why did she let herself be drawn into this stupid challenge? Simone hadn't worked out on the stair climber for weeks. Her calves cried for mercy and her quads begged her to stop. Gritting her teeth against the agony, she looked over to find Gabe staring at her.

What was with this guy? Did everything have to be a competition? This was worse than her and Eva, battling over whose turn it was to do the dishes or clean the bathrooms. They'd fought over everything, challenging each other in various ways to see who had to do which chores. Eva was bigger and stronger, but Simone was wiry and quick. Olivia had always been tiny and frail, even as a toddler. They kept her out of their scuffles.

She couldn't lose Olivia. There had to be a cure for her rare form of cancer. A slow-growing glioma, her dad said. Simone still felt the sting of betrayal that her parents hadn't told her of Olivia's seizures and the results of her MRI.

"We didn't want to worry you," Mom had said.

Now the worry was magnified by knowing her little sister could die.

Gabe's voice interrupted her thoughts. "You okay?"

"Yeah, sure. Why wouldn't I be?"

"Your face kinda tightened," Gabe said. "Like a frown."

"Maybe I'm frowning because you're …" Simone couldn't finish the sentence. She didn't want to be rude, but sometimes the words exploded from her mouth before she could stop them. She and her friend Mariah had that in common.

Simone punched the buttons to stop the machine.

"Quitting already?" Gabe asked.

"I'll be right back." Simone ignored the tight muscles in her legs and strode into the supply room. Grabbing two towels, she headed back to the stair machines.

"Here." She handed Gabe a towel and climbed back on the stair machine.

"Thanks." He wiped the towel across his face.

"We're over halfway finished," Simone said, looking at the timer. "How are you doing?"

"Worried?" Gabe asked with a grin.

Simone rolled her eyes. "Your safety is my responsibility. I need to make sure you're not going to pass out."

Gabe's breath came in short gasps. "I'm okay."

"What's your heart rate?"

Gabe touched his smart watch. "One fifty."

Simone did a quick calculation before reaching over and slowing the pace of Gabe's machine. "Let's take it down a notch."

"I said I'm okay."

"Stop being stubborn. I'm the professional here." Sheesh. The last thing she wanted was a repeat of Monday's workout.

"Fine," Gabe muttered.

Simone had no doubt she'd feel this workout tomorrow. That was one thing she missed as a trainer. The sore muscles from a hard workout. Working with clients and helping in the gym didn't leave her time for her own personal training. Maybe she should find something like what Gabe was doing—a goal to work towards. Like a marathon. She'd read about an event in California called Tough Mudder. It was an extreme challenge through an obstacle course designed to test one's stamina, strength, and mental grit.

Her thoughts returned to the Camino de Santiago. There was no way she'd do the trip alone. If she could find a couple of friends to go with, that would be something to work towards. She'd heard the Camino was more than a trek through the mountains of Spain. It was also a spiritual journey, which was something she could use. Especially in light of her sister's illness.

Gabe's voice interrupted her musing. "You're still going with me to the concert tonight, right?"

She'd totally forgotten that she'd agreed to go out with him. Simone bit her lip.

She felt his eyes studying her.

"Don't go thinking you're going to bail on me," Gabe said with a frown.

That was exactly what she was thinking.

"After forcing me to endure this torture, the least you can do is honor your commitment."

Simone's shoulders tightened. "Honor my commitment? What kind of comment is that?"

Gabe shrugged as his machine slowed, indicating the end of the time set. "You said you'd go to the concert with me tonight. Did I assume wrong that you are a person who keeps her promises?"

Simone stepped off the stair machine and stood with her hands on her hips. "I keep my promises."

Gabe's grin had the dual effect of infuriating her and making her want to smile back. She studied him for a moment, taking in the deepening tan which set off his blue eyes. The guy was cute. She'd give him that. But super annoying.

"Good," Gabe said. "Because I don't want to have to resort to bribing you with another Fluffy's double scoop."

Simone chuckled. "Oh, you *will* buy me ice cream, mister. No ice cream, no date. Are we clear?"

Gabe sent her a mock salute. "Yes, ma'am."

"Good. Let's cool down and stretch."

~

Lizzy called while Simone drove home from the gym to shower and change.

"Want to do a girl's movie night?" Lizzy asked. "Roman is out of town and Abby is spending the night with a friend."

Simone sucked in a breath through clenched teeth. The last thing she wanted was a grilling from her bestie about her date. "I can't. I'm going to the concert."

"Oh, come on, play with me. I'm bored."

Simone ran her tongue over her teeth. "I, um, actually have a date."

Lizzy's quick inhale was followed by a squeal. "With Carl? A second date?"

"Uh, no. With Gabe Harrison."

"Your Glory Hog? No way!"

"Yes, way."

"I thought you hated his guts?"

"I don't hate him. That wouldn't be Christian. I just, well, I don't know how to put this." How to tell Lizzy she'd felt so guilty about working Gabe too hard on Monday that she'd agreed to go out with him.

"You like him now?" Lizzy asked.

"I don't dislike him." Much.

Lizzy was silent for several beats. "Are you okay, Simone?" Lizzy's concern oozed through the phone.

Simone pulled into her apartment parking lot and turned off the car. "I'm okay. I'll tell you and Mariah all about it on Sunday, okay?"

"Seriously? You're going to make me wait until Sunday to find out what's going on?"

"I'm sorry. I really am. It's a lot to digest right now." Simone removed her phone from the holder. "And I have to go get ready for my date."

Lizzy sighed. "Fine. But you better be prepared to spill, girlfriend. Call me tomorrow and tell me how your date went with Glory Hog."

Simone smiled. "Sure."

"Wear something cute," Lizzy said as she disconnected.

'Something cute' ended up being a pair of jeans and a tee shirt. Her wardrobe was in desperate need of a makeover. She'd mention it to Mariah when they met on Sunday evening. Mariah loved to shop and would jump at the chance to help.

As long as Mariah didn't make her buy a pair of ankle-breakers. That kind of shoe came with a huge price tag.

While she waited for Gabe, Simone sent a text to her sister.

Simone: How are you feeling?

Bubble appeared showing Olivia was thumbing a response.

Olivia: I'm 18. I have MS and a brain tumor. HOW DO YOU THINK I'M FEELING???

Simone grimaced. It *was* a dumb question. She considered several responses and rejected each one, including 'I'm praying for you.' She opted for an attempt at humor.

Simone: Think of all the chores you'll get out of. (smiley face)

Olivia: Ha ha.

Simone: You know there are easier ways to get attention, right?

Olivia: Now you tell me.

Satisfied for the moment Olivia would be okay, Simone sat on the couch to wait for her date.

~

Gabe found his mom in the backyard watching Grace's girls splash in the wading pool. Grace lay in the shade nearby, reading a paperback.

"Hi, honey. How was your workout?"

Gabe leaned down to drop a kiss on his mom's cheek. "It was fine."

"You're going to have to do better than that, Gabriel."

Gabe dropped onto the grass and leaned back on his arms. "It was grueling," he admitted. "I had to do the stair climber for thirty minutes with a fifty-pound pack on my back," He rolled his shoulders up and back, remembering the weight. "My trainer is a sadist."

Mom's face wrinkled with concern. "Are you sure you should be doing this? It sounds hard."

"Mom, stop. I carry that much weight in gear when

we go out on a call."

His mom's eyebrows rose. "I had no idea."

Gabe nodded. "Yup. I don't always have to climb stairs for thirty minutes."

Mom shook her head with a smile. "Okay, if you say so. If you're hungry, I made some sandwiches. They're in the fridge. Tonight, we're all fending for ourselves. I'm too tired to cook and it's too hot."

"No problem, Mom. I'll grab a sandwich on my way out."

"Where ya going?" Grace asked, lowering her sunglasses.

"Hot August Nights concert."

"Sounds fun," Grace said. "Wish I could go. Who else is going?"

Gabe swallowed. "Uh, I'm not sure."

Grace sent him a sly smile. She knew him too well. "You have a date, don't you?"

Mom's smile stretched across her face. "A date? Anyone I know?"

Gabe had hoped to avoid the grilling he was sure to get from Mom and Grace. Why did women need to know every single detail?

"Her name is Simone Coleman."

Grace tapped a finger against her lips. "Where have I heard that name before?" Grace snapped her fingers. "Isn't she a personal trainer at Gym Time?"

Gabe didn't answer. He could see the wheels turning in his sister's head.

"What a minute," Grace said. "She's *your* personal trainer."

Mom's head swiveled his direction. "Isn't that some sort of conflict of interest?"

Grace sent him a teasing grin. "What kind of workout do you have planned for her tonight, Gabe?"

"Grace!" Mom admonished her. "None of that kind of talk. Gabe knows what the Bible teaches."

Mom's words sent a knife blade of guilt into Gabe's gut. Good thing she never knew about Tiffany and his resulting fall into sexual sin.

"On that note, ladies, I'm going to go inside and shower." Gabe lumbered to his feet and groaned. His legs felt like a rubber hose that had lain in the sun too long. A nice hot shower would help loosen up his muscles.

He strode into the house on the heels of Grace's laughter.

Chapter 17

Simone paced from the kitchen to the living room window while she waited for Gabe to pull into the parking lot. After a drought of no dates since Adam, now she had a date two Fridays in a row. Go figure.

Gabe pulled to a stop and Simone watched him slide out of his pickup. His gait was slow as he approached her front door. Probably as sore as she was from the stair machine.

Her phone rang and she answered without looking at the screen, putting it on speaker.

"Hello?" Simone opened the door and motioned for Gabe to enter.

"Hi, Simone. This is Carl."

Simone pinched her lips together. She should have looked at the phone first.

Carl's voice boomed. "Sorry to call late, but duty calls me to patrol tonight's concert. My way of giving back to the community, you know. I'll make a point to say hi, if you're going."

Carl paused. Was he waiting for some words of affirmation?

"Okay." Simone glanced at Gabe, who stood in the doorway jingling his keys in one hand. Dang the guy was good looking.

"I'm off tomorrow, though. Would you like to grab some dinner?"

"Tomorrow?" Simone felt herself go warm. Gabe in her doorway and Carl on the phone. How to decline his offer while Gabe's mouth stretched into a grin.

Gabe made a slashing motion with his finger across his neck.

"Uh, Carl, hold on a moment." She put the phone on mute. "What?"

"Before you commit to Carl the Cop, I wanted to ask you if you'd come to my house tomorrow afternoon. I've invited a couple of people over to cheer up my sister."

Talk about a difficult decision. Dinner with Carl or time spent with Glory. "Uh, Carl, I can't tomorrow."

"What about Sunday? We could take a drive to the coast or something."

Simone tried to put the right amount of apology in her voice. "I spend Sunday with my parents in Salem."

"Okay. I get it. Thanks anyway." Carl did not sound happy.

Simone grimaced as she disconnected.

"Everything okay?" Gabe asked with a smile.

"Peachy." Simone grabbed a hoodie and her purse. "Let's go, okay?"

"I'm planning to surprise my sister by having a couple of friends over. She's going crazy having to take it easy for these last few weeks."

"I can imagine. I remember spraining my ankle and having to use crutches for a few weeks. No running, walking, or working out."

"Were you doing anything fun?"

"To cause the sprain?" Simone grimaced. "It was stupid. Lizzy and I decided to float down the Willamette River on inner tubes. I hopped out to head onto the shore and slipped on some loose rocks." She flexed her foot, remembering the searing pain from rolling her ankle.

"Ouch."

Gabe snagged a parking spot two blocks away. The concert venue was beginning to fill when they arrived. Gabe waved at a couple of his friends. Simone saw Mariah and Ethan in the distance, but they seemed engaged in a deep conversation. More than likely discussing their upcoming wedding. She bit her lip, remembering she'd committed to being a bridesmaid. If she moved to Beaverton, her duties would have to be accomplished long distance. Ugh.

She and Gabe found seats near the back and settled in to wait.

"Thanks for agreeing to come to my parents' house tomorrow. Grace gets super bored sitting all day."

"When is she due?"

"The end of August."

"Right before you go back," Simone commented.

The music started and Simone settled in to listen to the opening warm-up band. They were a local bluegrass band and were pretty good. Forty minutes later, they wrapped up with a soulful tune that brought tears to Simone's eyes. It was a song about family and relationships. She used her fingertips to wipe away tears.

Gabe leaned toward her, brushing his shoulder against hers. "Are you okay?"

Simone nodded with a gulp. "That was beautiful."

Gabe stared into her eyes. "Want to talk about it?"

How was he able to read her mind? Simone shook her head. If she brought up Olivia's name, she'd start blubbering. Not a good look on a first date.

"I'm fine."

"If you say so," Gabe responded. "I'll be right back. Will you be okay by yourself for a minute?"

"Sure." His absence would give her a chance to compose herself. Simone watched as Gabe approached a group of guys. She recognized some of them from the Main Fire Department. There was a lot of backslapping and fist-bumping among the men.

"Hey, I hoped I'd see you here." Carl's greeting caught her midbreath.

Simone's throat tightened. "Oh, hi."

Carl rested his hands on his duty belt. His eyes roamed around the crowd before coming to rest on her.

"How are you enjoying the concert so far?" he asked.

"It's good."

"I'm surprised to see such a pretty lady sitting by herself." Carl grinned down at her.

Simone resisted the urge to roll her eyes.

Carl shifted his weight onto the balls of his feet. "Well, I better get back to patrolling. Duty calls. See you around."

"Yeah, see you."

Carl gave a mock salute before turning and striding toward the beer garden.

Simone took a couple of deep breaths, held them for ten seconds and blew them out. By the time Gabe came back to his seat, she'd calmed her emotions.

"How's Carl the cop?" Gabe asked.

Simone shook her head. "Annoying."

Gabe laughed.

After a few minutes, the second act began their set. They were a punk rock type band with lots of screeching guitars and screaming voices.

Simone cringed. If she was here with Lizzy, they would have exchanged a look and silently agreed to leave.

Gabe leaned over and yelled in her ear. "They're terrible. Want to get out of here?"

~

Gabe couldn't believe she said yes to leaving. Once they were out of earshot, the music became white noise in the background.

"I promised you Fluffy's, didn't I?" he asked. "Let's go."

Gabe grabbed her hand, surprised that she didn't pull away. When they got to Fluffy's mobile truck, the line had gone down to two people.

"What flavor do you want?"

"I think you mean flavors. With an S." Simone said, eyeing the choices posted on the chalkboard.

"Two scoops?" Gabe asked, raising his eyebrows.

"Or three. Long week. Difficult clients."

"Ha. I see how you are." They stepped to the window to place their orders. "I'll have a scoop of chocolate cookie dough and one of mint chip." He turned to Simone. "Have you decided?"

She sent him a look he couldn't decipher. "I'll have the same."

Gabe raised his eyebrows. "*Only* two scoops?"

Simone nodded. Gabe dropped her hand to reach into his pocket for his wallet. He paid and they stepped aside to wait for their cones.

Cones in hand, they strolled down the sidewalk toward the Courthouse square. Gabe pointed to a bench under the shade of some oak trees. "Want to sit?"

"Sure."

Once they were seated, Gabe asked, "What has you worried?"

Simone sent him a sideways glance. "What makes you think I'm worried about something?"

Gabe snorted. "It's written all over your face."

He heard her deep sigh. "It's my sister. She has a brain tumor."

Gabe fumbled with his cone. "That's scary. I can't begin to imagine how worried you must be. I'm worried about my sister having a healthy baby."

"My parents are moving to North Dakota to be near a treatment center. I don't know whether to go with them or stay here."

"The Roger Maris Cancer Center?"

Simone shot a glance his way. "You know about that?"

"Of course. The center is one of the premier cancer centers in the US. Our team did a fund-raiser every year for the families who stayed nearby while their kids, spouses, whatever, went through treatments. Like a Ronald McDonald House." Gabe paused to catch a drip down the side of his cone. "What made your parents pick that one? I mean, Fargo, North Dakota is pretty remote."

"My dad played ball."

"No way. What position? Did he go pro?"

"He blew out his ankle sliding into home base during his senior year."

Gabe nodded. "What's his name? I'm gonna have to look him up."

"Cassius. Same last name as me."

"That's so cool." Gabe leaned back on the bench. "I'm dating a college ball player's daughter."

Simone chuckled. "It's one date, Glory. Don't get ahead of yourself."

We'll see, Simone. "So, what else is bugging you?"

Simone paused to catch some drips with her tongue. "I have a job offer in Beaverton which I'm supposed to decide on soon." She sent him a small smile. "And I have this really difficult client I'm working with."

Gabe chuckled. "That's definitely the worst." He sobered and laid a hand on her thigh. "I'm sorry about your sister. How old is she?"

"Eighteen. My parents have never said this, but I think she was an 'oops' baby. She's ten years younger than me."

"Do you have any other siblings?"

"My older sister, Eva. You might have crossed paths with her in high school."

Gabe tried to picture a younger version of Simone from his teenage years. He would have noticed someone around his age who was a mix of Black and White.

"When did she graduate?" Gabe asked.

"I think the year after you. She was a junior when I was a freshman." Simone took a bite of her ice cream and spoke around the mouthful. "She doesn't look anything like me. She takes after our mom."

That explained why Gabe couldn't place her. "I was pretty much self-absorbed in high school, so I wouldn't have paid much attention to anyone in a lower grade."

"Some things never change, do they?"

"Ouch. Your sarcasm wounds me."

Simone smiled behind her ice cream cone. "Truth hurts, Glory."

Gabe bumped his shoulder against hers. "I'm sorry about that." And he was. It was time to let everyone know Simone's part in the rescue of the motorcyclist.

"Did I tell you I found out the guy on the bike is going to be okay?"

Simone half-turned toward him. "He is? That's great."

Gabe stared into her eyes and felt himself falling. His mouth went dry as he tried to absorb what that meant. His mind flashed to Tiffany and he quickly shoved the thought away. Simone was as different from her as water was to fire. The silence lengthened as they held each other's gaze.

He sucked in a breath. "Uh, yeah. I talked to some first responders, and they told me he was out of the hospital."

Simone seemed unaware of the rivulets of ice cream dripping down the side of her cone and onto her hand.

She shook her head, snapping herself out of her silence. "I guess I need a napkin," she said, licking her fingers.

Gabe pulled a wad from his shirt pocket and handed them to her. Simone did the best she could to wipe the sticky mess from her hand before shrugging. Gabe admired her nonchalance. Tiffany would have pitched a hissy fit in the same situation.

They finished their cones, crunching on the last pointy bite.

"I could live on this stuff," Simone said.

"Definitely." Gabe struggled to find something to say. Anything to get Simone talking again. "When do you have to decide on the job offer?"

Simone stared across the quad into the distance. The trees overhead moved and swayed in the evening breeze, bringing a needed drop in the summer temperature.

"I have to go up to Beaverton next week and at least check out the place. My old college friend, DavidJon opened a boutique gym there. He wants me to come on board as a trainer."

"Is that what you want?"

Simone shrugged. "I think so. I'd like to go somewhere different. Travel. Make more money."

"What about North Dakota?"

Simone looked down at her hands, clasped in her lap. "I could go with my folks, but I'd have to find a job there." Her hands formed fists and she pounded them on her thighs. "I don't know what to do."

Gabe leaned back and stretched out his legs, crossing them at the ankles. "I applied for a job in South Carolina."

Simone's head swiveled to his. "Really? Why South Carolina?"

"Like you, I wanted to try someplace else." He raised one shoulder. "Escape."

Simone regarded him for a moment. "Escape. I know the feeling. Did you get the job?"

Gabe swallowed his disappointment. "Nope."

"That stinks. So, you're going back to Portland to your old station?"

"Yup. My captain wants to quote 'have a talk' when I get back."

"That sounds ominous."

"I think he's disappointed because I haven't tried testing for a higher position."

"Why not?"

How to answer? Should he dump the Tiffany situation on Simone, or was it not something he should share on a first date? It could go either way. She could show grace, as a Christian should, or she could judge him for being a sinful wretch.

Gabe wanted Simone's approval and maybe even her affection. What he felt for her did not compare to his feelings for Tiffany. That had been attraction based on lust. He'd been as guilty as Tiffany for what they'd done.

Perhaps some deep soul-searching was needed, along with a healthy dose of prayer. Gabe took a deep breath and exhaled slowly.

Chapter 18

Simone held her breath. What could he want to escape from? And how did that impact his reasons for not trying for a promotion?

Simone watched the emotions play over his face. He'd dropped his usual grin. A muscle worked in his jaw. She resisted the urge to lay a hand on his cheek.

"There's something you should know," Gabe said. "About me."

Simone's heart sank. He was engaged. The budding attraction she felt would be crushed under a hundred-pound dumbbell. Why was she always attracted to guys who were emotionally unavailable? That's what happened with Adam. They'd gotten engaged without her realizing he had a secret agenda to move far away from Main. She'd tried to explain to him she couldn't leave her family. But he made plans anyway. The ultimatum he'd delivered still ached.

Adam pushed her into a corner. *You have to choose, Simone. Me or your parents.*

Adam couldn't understand her need to be close enough to support her folks after Olivia's diagnosis of MS.

Gabe shifted on the bench and leaned over, resting

his forearms on his thighs.

Simone's pulse sped up. "Go on."

"I was engaged once. We broke up several months ago."

Simone waited. There was more to the story. She took a second, relieved he wasn't currently engaged.

"We, uh …" He cleared his throat and sucked in a breath. "We were intimate. She got pregnant."

Blindsided by an emotional punching bag, she swallowed deep disappointment. Gabe had a kid somewhere? The growing attraction she felt would have to go on hold. She wasn't ready to take on the responsibility of someone else's child in addition to her current drama.

"She . . ."

Simone couldn't handle any more. She made a move to stand but his hand grabbed her arm.

"Wait. Let me finish."

Simone sat back. How much worse could it get?

"Tiffany, my ex-fiancée, terminated the pregnancy without telling me."

Simon gasped. "That's terrible!" Every fiber of Simone's being wanted to find this woman and yank her hair out. She glanced at Gabe and saw tears forming in his eyes. He looked gutted. She laid a hand on his cheek and gently pulled his face toward hers.

"I'm sorry."

Gabe's head dropped. His voice was hoarse. "You're the only other person who knows."

Simone absorbed the information. Why would he trust her enough to tell her something that personal? This changed the dynamic of their relationship. No longer were they trainer and client. The shift was subtle. They'd both shared their secrets and struggles and couldn't go back. Simone had thought Gabe was nothing more than an egocentric glory hog. She now saw him as another human, trying to make it in a confusing and often painful world.

~

Gabe dared to raise his eyes to Simone's when she laid her hand on his face. Her palm was warm and her eyes were filled with sympathy. He'd expected judgement and was shown mercy. The same attributes he'd been taught about God. His heart swelled with gratitude.

Gabe placed a hand over hers. "Thank you."

Without letting himself think, Gabe lowered his head to Simone's and laid his lips gently on hers. She inhaled before she returned the kiss. There were no fireworks. No spark of physical desire. But the kiss felt like coming home after a long journey. Like slipping off his steel-toed work boots at the end of a long day.

He pulled back to gauge her response. Simone's eyes were closed, and her face looked more relaxed than it had been all week. He kissed her again then leaned his forehead against hers.

"I'm not going to apologize," he said.

Simone's eyes flew open. She jerked away and turned to face the setting sun as it cast shadows on the grassy expanse. "This isn't going to work."

Gabe slumped against the back of the bench. "You're probably right."

Simone sent him a sideways smile. "Care to repeat that?"

He pushed himself to his feet and held out a hand. "I better get you home."

When Simone placed her hand in his, Gabe couldn't shake the same feeling he'd gotten when they'd kissed. She felt like home.

~

Simone couldn't help her disappointment that Gabe didn't try to argue when she said a relationship between them wouldn't work. He could have at least tried.

She stayed quiet when Gabe tried to engage her in conversation as they made their way to where he parked his truck.

"Thanks for sharing with me about your sister," he said.

"Sure."

"Keep me posted about her treatment, okay?"

"Okay."

She felt his eyes on her in the semidarkness. She crossed her arms over her chest to hold in the hurt. But that kiss. Wow. Simone hadn't felt a kiss like that before. Different from Adam's demanding lips. Gabe's were gentle, giving her a chance to respond before continuing.

"I'm sorry you're upset," Gabe said.

He pulled up in front of her apartment and turned off the ignition.

"You don't have to walk me to my door," Simone told him, grabbing for the handle.

Gabe grabbed her hand before she could escape. "Wait."

Simone pressed her lips together and paused.

"Just because I'm leaving at the end of the month, and you're going who-knows-where, doesn't mean we can't be friends. Does it?"

He looked so earnest that Simone almost felt sorry

for him. One corner of her mouth rose. "Friends?"

Gabe nodded.

"Friends don't kiss." She raised her eyebrows while he digested this fact.

She watched him work out the problem. Then his face broke out into a grin. "Okay. Friends. No kissing." He leaned toward her and placed a soft kiss on her lips. "That's to show you what you'll be missing."

Simone smacked his firm bicep. "Stop."

He raised his hands in surrender. "Fine. I'm done. Now, since we're friends and all, you'll come to my parents' house tomorrow and cheer up my sister, right?"

"Okay."

"And after that, if we decide to do something like, maybe, go to a movie, you'd be down with that? As friends might do on a Saturday night?"

Simone puffed a breath out of her nose. "We'll see."

"And then Sunday—"

"Don't press your luck, Glory."

Gabe leaned back and guffawed. "See you tomorrow. Three o'clock. I'll text you their address."

Simone let herself out of his pickup and slid to the pavement. When she reached her front door, she turned around to see Gabe waiting for her to unlock the door and go in. She waved goodbye and turned to open the door, keys in hand. She heard the truck pull away with a muffled roar when she turned on the living room light.

She dropped her purse on her bed and sank on the edge, letting her head droop. The evening hadn't turned out anything like she'd expected. Her intention had been to go on one pity date with the guy, then make excuses as to why she couldn't see him again.

He was her client.

He was leaving at the end of the month.

Her life was too uncertain.

Now she had a new friend when she wanted more than friendship. Who would have thought? But she'd set herself up for another round of hurt. Friends. Yeah, no.

Simone changed into pajamas and slipped into bed to check her social media. Before she could log onto Instagram, her phone dinged with a text.

Gabe: Hope you sleep well. Thanks for a great evening. Friend.

Simone: My friends know I'm an early riser, so no texting this late

Gabe: I guess I have some work to do to get to know my new friend

Simone: Slow learner, are you?

Gabe: You wound me. Is that how friends are supposed to treat each other?

Simone: Goodnight, Glory

Gabe: LOL

Chapter 19

Gabe propped his feet on the back porch railing and sipped his second cup of coffee. The silence was interrupted only by the melodic chirping of birds, greeting the morning. He had approximately thirty minutes before Grace's twin hurricanes woke up. A plume of dust rose into the cerulean colored sky from his dad's combine, too far away to be heard. A few puffy clouds dotted the horizon.

Gabe's mom stepped through the back door and sank into a chair next to him. "Looks like it's going to be another beautiful day."

Gabe felt a stab of guilt that he wasn't already in the field helping his dad. "I'll go out and see what Dad needs." He made a move to get up, but his mom laid a hand on his arm.

"Don't go yet. I hardly get a chance to talk to you by myself."

Gabe settled back with a sigh of relief. Moments like this were rare. In Portland, his workdays started with chaos and often ended the same. Twelve-hour shifts followed by days making up for lost sleep.

"I can't thank you enough for coming down to help us," Mom said. "I hope your work is okay with you being gone for this month."

Gabe shrugged. "They're not thrilled. But I told them family comes first."

Mom took a sip of her coffee. "I'll bet you'll be glad to go back," she said with a smile. "It isn't easy coming home. Especially with two noisy toddlers."

"It's okay. I'm enjoying being around all of you. I didn't realize how much I've missed coming home."

Mom reached over and grasped his hand. "I'm glad."

Gabe watched the combine move closer. "I applied for a job out of state."

His mom's quick inhale spoke more than any words.

"I didn't get the job." Gabe said quickly.

"Where?"

"South Carolina."

"But that's clear across the country! Does this have anything to do with Tiffany."

It had everything to do with Tiffany, but Gabe wasn't ready to tell his mother. "In a way, yes."

Mom was silent for several beats. "I never liked her. I'm sorry."

Gabe reached out an arm and squeezed his mom's shoulder. "It's okay, Mom." He glanced up to the rumble of the combine approaching the house.

"I never told you this, Gabriel, but she made a nasty comment about your sister's marriage to Demarcus." Mom's eyes filled with tears. "You know we never raised you and Grace to be prejudiced. But that woman." Mom's voice shook. "She said something vile about your sister marrying a Black man."

Gabe blew out a breath. "Oh my gosh." Why was he

not surprised?

The combine ground to a halt and Gabe's dad climbed down from the cab.

"Did you save me any of that coffee?" He strode to the porch and dropped a kiss on Gabe's mom's head. She smiled up at him.

Gabe envied their relationship. In his heart, he longed for a good woman's love. A partner who would fearlessly join him in the battle of life's adversities. His parents' lives hadn't been easy. They'd experienced the death of a child. His brother would have been older than Grace, but he'd died at only a few months of age. His mom still grew sad as the day of his death approached.

Recalling their grief brought Simone's situation to mind. If her sister died, how would her parents deal with their grief? How would Simone deal with the loss?

His dad returned to the porch with a steaming mug of coffee. "You ready to get to work, lazybones?"

Mom swatted his arm. "Leave him alone, John. I've been having a nice conversation with our son."

"We're burning daylight, Debbie."

"I know, I know. Drink your coffee and I'll make us some breakfast."

Gabe stopped her with his hand. "I invited a couple of people over this afternoon to hang out. I thought we might cheer Grace up."

"Oh, sweetie, that's so thoughtful. Thank you. Who is coming?"

"A couple of Grace's friends from church." Gabe swallowed. "And Simone Coleman."

Mom raised her brows until they disappeared at the bottom of her bangs. "Simone the personal trainer? The one I heard you complaining about to Grace?"

Gabe felt his face grow hot. "We've called a truce."

Mom stared at him with a knowing look. "Really?"

"We're friends, mom. Just friends."

Mom pursed her lips before breaking into a grin. "Right." She disappeared into the house before he could protest.

Dad sank into the chair his mom had vacated. "Anything going on I should know about?"

Gabe drained the last of his brew. "Nope."

Dad leveled his gaze on him. "Friends or no, I'm sure you'll treat her with the utmost respect. Remember what we taught you. Treat girls like you would want your sister to be treated."

The shame Gabe tried to ignore came back to rest heavily on his shoulders. He hadn't treated Tiffany like his sister and that had turned out to be a dumpster fire.

Time to confess and hopefully find the grace he desperately needed from his dad.

"Dad, there's something you should know."

~

Simone headed to Gym Time early Saturday to take advantage of the relative un-busyness of the gym on a weekend morning. After a ten-minute warm up on the recumbent bike, she headed into the large room to punish the punching bag.

There was something cleansing about beating the heck out of the leather bag. She knew all the so-called therapeutic benefits of getting out your aggressions. But for Simone, it was about pushing her body to its limit.

Goosebumps mixed with sweat broke out as she remembered Gabe's kiss.

Jab, parry, right hook, left undercut. Repeat. The

repetition gave her mind a chance to work through the problem of Gabe.

His kiss had awakened something in her that had been dormant since Adam. Simone thought the feelings had died. She was wrong. They were merely lying dormant, waiting for . . . Gabe?

The thought confounded her. Sure, he was cute. And he had great legs. He was fun and funny. But his ego. It was too big for the little town of Main.

Out of breath, Simone bent over to steady her breathing. She was no closer to figuring out what to do about Gabe than when she started. He wanted to be friends. How could she be friends with him after that kiss? Simone wanted more. But he was leaving in a couple of weeks.

For Simone, a kiss meant a promise. An intimate act stating an intention. Once it happened, you couldn't go backwards. It wasn't like throwing your car in reverse.

With a groan, Simone stripped off her gloves and headed home to shower. She'd hoped to have some idea of her direction for the future, but all her pondering had been in Gabe's direction.

Darn him. Now she had to go meet his family and play nice with his sister.

Her phone rang as she stepped into her apartment.

"Granny! How are you? I'm sorry I haven't called you in a while." Simone's momentary guilt eased when her grandmother responded.

"It's fine, sugar. I'm calling to see how you're doing?" Granny's tissue paper voice revealed her advancing years.

Simone sank sideways onto her couch and stretched out her legs. "You've talked to Dad."

"Of course, honey. He called me directly after Olivia's diagnosis. Tsk. Such a burden for a young girl."

Olivia's throat clogged with unshed tears. "What are we going to do, Granny?"

"The same as we always do, Sugar. We cast our cares on the Lord."

Simone had always been amazed at Granny's calm acceptance of God's will. Her faith never wavered, unlike Simone's. "How do you do it, Granny?"

Granny chuckled. "Years of experience. But you tell me what's happening in your world. This call is about you."

Simone shared everything that had happened since witnessing the motorcycle accident. Granny was the one person who listened without interruption and without judgement.

When Simone wound down, Granny asked. "How much time have you spent praying over all this?"

Count on her grandmother to get to the heart. "Not enough."

"Well, then." Granny's voice held a question.

"Okay, Granny. I promise I'll spend some quality time with God."

"That's my girl. Now you better let this old lady go and take her nap. I love you dearly, child."

"I love you too, Granny."

Chapter 20

Simone pulled into Gabe's parents' driveway and crunched over the gravel until she came to a stop on a concrete pad. Two other vehicles sat side by side. One was Gabe's white pickup. The other she didn't recognize.

The front door opened, and Gabe stepped onto the porch. Her breath caught at the sight of him filling the door.

"You made it. I thought you might ghost me."

Simone sent him a close-mouthed smile. "Is that what your friends do?"

Gabe laughed. "Not my real friends." He swung the door open and motioned for her to come in. "Everyone is out back."

Simone studied the comfortable living room and open floor plan. A worn-looking sofa had a knit afghan tossed over the back cushions. Two recliners faced the huge flat-screen television mounted on one wall. A bookshelf held what looked like a gaming station and several books. A few framed photos were scattered around. Simone didn't have time to register the people in the photos before Gabe whisked her into the kitchen.

"Want anything to drink?" he asked, his hand on the

doorknob leading out to the backyard.

"I'm good."

"I need to warn you, my nieces are hyped up over having company. They can be a little overwhelming at times."

"Who else is here?"

"Vivian and Nicolas. They're friends of my sister."

Simone nodded. She didn't recall them, but that didn't matter. Gabe swung open the back door and let her pass. Simone stepped onto the back porch and took in the scene.

Gabe's sister was easy to pick out. She sat on a lounger with her legs stretched out. Her swollen belly pressed against the maternity top. Two people sat in chairs on one side of her, facing the trampoline, where two little girls bounced and giggled.

They stopped when they spied Simone and Gabe and returned to bouncing. Simone stared at the twins, aghast.

She'd expected two little light-skinned, light-haired cherubs. Like Gabe. Like Grace. Simone swiveled her head to Gabe's sister. Brown hair tumbled beneath a floppy hat, partially covering fair skin. Her head swiveled back to the girls.

Simone grabbed Gabe's arm. "Is your sister—"

"Yes, she's about ready to pop," Gabe said with a grimace.

"No, is she married—"

"Of course she's married. We don't, well, some of us don't, you know . . ." Gabe's voice trailed off. His revelation last night had been painful to hear.

Gabe linked his arm in hers. "Come on, I'll introduce you."

Grace smiled when Gabe approached. "So, this is the cruel taskmaster my brother complains about."

Simone sent Gabe the stink-eye. "Really?"

Gabe spread his hands out. "Truth hurts."

Gabe pulled up two more lawn chairs as Grace introduced Simone to her friends.

"When are you due?" Simone asked.

Grace rubbed her pregnancy bump. "If I'm able to go full-term, September 3. I'm praying he doesn't want to make an early appearance. I'd really like my husband to be here." She cast a wistful look at the girls, who'd clambered down from the trampoline and were chasing each other around. "He didn't get to be here for their birth."

"Where is he, if you don't mind my asking?

"He's in Germany. Air Force. He's supposed to take leave in a couple of weeks." Grace shrugged. "But you know the government."

Simone nodded as if she understood, but no one in her family had served in the military.

She wanted to probe but couldn't find questions to ask that wouldn't sound awkward. 'Is your husband Black?' was probably not the right thing to say on their first meeting.

A few minutes later, an older version of Grace came outside and called to the twins.

"Hope, Mercy, come get some water." The girls scampered to the porch, and each grabbed a plastic tumbler.

"Mom, come meet Simone," Gabe said.

Simone's apprehension at meeting Gabe's mother dissipated as soon as Debbie pulled her into a warm hug. "I'm pleased to meet some of Gabe's friends."

"It's nice to meet you too." Simone smiled into the older woman's eyes. They were the same blue as Gabe's.

"I haven't seen you at church. Do you attend Main Community?"

Simone shook her head. "No, I drive to Salem on Sunday and go to church with my family."

"How sweet. Family is important, especially as we get older. Do you have brothers and sisters?"

"Two sisters. One is older and she has triplets. My younger sister still lives at home."

"Triplets! My, that must be a challenge. Grace has her hands full with two."

~

Gabe watched his mom and Simone chat as if they'd known each other for years. Something inside him shifted. He didn't want to be friends with Simone. He wanted more. When he'd kissed her last night, he expected her to either recoil in disgust or punch him in the face. Instead, she'd kissed him back before declaring, 'this won't work.'

He wanted to grab her arm and pull her away from the group. Go somewhere remote where he could get to know her. Find out her deepest longings, her worst fears, her desire for the future. If there was any possibility she wanted the same things he did, there might be a future for the two of them. Together.

A spark of jealousy burned into flame as he watched Nicolas staring at Simone. The feeling was ridiculous. Nicolas and Vivian were married. But still, why was he staring intently as Simone answered Nicolas's questions.

"You work at Gym Time?" Nicolas asked.

"I'm a personal trainer."

Gabe inserted himself into the conversation. "She's my personal trainer. I'm training for the 9/11 stair challenge."

"What is that?" Vivian asked.

"It's a way for first responders to honor the ones who made the ultimate sacrifice on September 11. I believe it's important to memorialize their deaths."

Simone sent him an amused glance. He sounded pompous but he didn't care.

"Speaking of first responders," Grace interjected, "Nicolas, whatever happened to that guy whose life Gabe saved. The motorcycle guy?"

Nicolas leaned forward and rested his arms on his thighs. "He was released from the hospital a few days ago. Can you believe all he suffered was a broken wrist?"

"That's incredible," Grace said.

Nicolas chuckled. "Well, that and a bruised chest from your brother's enthusiastic CPR."

Gabe's eyes swung to Simone when she cleared her throat. She turned her gaze on him with hooded eyes.

"Yeah, about that," Gabe said. "I wasn't actually the first one on the scene."

Nicolas sat up straight and snapped his fingers. "That's where I know you from." He pointed at Simone. "You were at the accident. I looked for you after we loaded the victim into the ambulance, but you were gone."

Before Simone could answer, Grace's girls dashed toward the group and began pestering his sister.

"Come play with us, Mommy. Please."

Gabe felt a combination of relief and guilt at the

interruption. By the time his mom gathered the girls and took them into the house, the conversation changed direction.

Grace covered her mouth to disguise a yawn.

"We should get going," Vivian said.

"Me too," Simone added.

"Help me up, Gabe," Grace said, extending her arm.

Gabe pulled her to an upright position and helped her to her feet.

"It's nap time," Grace said. She hugged her friends. "Thanks for coming. Please don't hesitate to come again. I get bored out of my skull lying around all day."

Nicolas turned to Simone. "I hope I see you at the City Council meeting next week. I'll make sure they know to honor you as well as Gabe here."

Gabe couldn't read Simone's expression. "Don't leave yet," he whispered. "Please."

Simone shot him a glare but returned to her lounge chair. Gabe helped his sister into the house and returned to the backyard with two bottles of water dripping with condensation.

"It's warm out here," Gabe said.

Simone opened her water and took a couple of sips without responding.

"Thanks for coming today. It meant a lot to Grace. And me."

Gabe glanced sideways trying to read Simone's expression.

"Is all this yours?" Simone asked, waving an arm toward the fields of grass seed.

"My parents', but yes."

Gabe mentally picked his way through several roads of conversation. Was she mad? He'd heard his married friends say that if their wives were upset, the best thing to do is apologize.

"Hey, I'm sorry."

Simone pinned him with her gaze. "Sorry for what?"

Gabe gulped. "Uh, for, you know, the …" His voice trailed off.

Simone made a snort of disgust. "You're too predictable, Glory. You can't even share one bit of the attention you're getting from saving that guys life." The air quotes she used enhanced her sarcasm.

How could he explain so she'd understand that his ego had been stomped and left gasping for air by his former girlfriend. He wanted, no, *needed* the affirmation of his peers that he was worthy of something—anything. True, Simone had played a part in helping save the motorcyclist's life. But if Gabe hadn't come along, what would have happened?

His conscience bit him in the backside. Would it hurt to share a tiny bit of the recognition?

Simone shot to her feet. "I need to go. Thanks for inviting me. Tell you mom I enjoyed meeting her."

Simone was halfway around the side of the house before Gabe stood. He dashed to catch up with her.

"Wait."

Simone stopped and turned. "What?"

"Want to go grab something to eat?" That wasn't what he'd planned to say. He'd wanted to pull Simone into a hug and explain.

Simone shook her head. "No thanks. I have a lot to do."

Gabe's mouth was dry, the taste of dust lingering on his tongue as he watched her drive away. He swallowed, trying to quell the lump in his throat as he struggled to find the right words to express his feelings. But it was too late. The plume of dust left in her wake drifted to the ground.

Chapter 21

Simone spent the rest of Saturday catching up on laundry and cleaning. Such was the life of a single woman on weekend. A few months ago, she'd have been out with Adam, having dinner with his friends.

With Mariah engaged to her youth pastor, and Lizzy comfortably settled into married life, Simone was the odd man out. She could drive into Salem and hang out with her family, but that would mean two trips in a row. Too exhausting.

Instead, she was home obsessing over Glory Hog. Why was he such a jerk? Why did she like him so much? What did it mean to be just friends?

Goosebumps rose on her arms when she remembered their kiss.

Stop. There would be no more kissing in their friendship. She remembered the line in the movie Princess Bride, "Is this a kissing book?"

Simone dumped the laundry basket on the bed. Before she could start folding the clothes, her cell phone pinged.

Gabe: Are will still friends? This was followed by a smiley face.

Simone typed out a response, then backspaced.

Tapping the phone on her lips, she tried to come up with something that wouldn't sound petulant.

Simone: Maybe

That would have to do.

Gabe: Is your friendship conditional

Simone sighed. Gabe was a pain in her backside but she didn't have to be.

Simone: No

Gabe: Good. Because friends don't let friends

The text ended. Simone stared at the screen, waiting for the rest of the text. There were no bubbles indicating he was composing a response. She waited a full minute. Nothing. She tossed the phone on the bed with a grunt.

Later that night as she prepared for bed, her phone pinged again.

Gabe: Sorry about that. Grace started having contractions. Had to call 911. She's okay but doc wants to see her Monday

Simone's heart stuttered.

Simone: Glad she's okay. I'll be praying

Gabe responded with a thumbs up emoji and **Tnx**.

When church let out the next day, Simone took time to chat with some of her parents' friends. The congregation was mostly people their age, with a few young married couples mixed in. Simone regretted not getting to know any of the singles in the church. With her two besties living their happily-ever-after lives, she was increasingly reminded of her single status.

Adam had been her ticket out of loneliness, but God had other plans for her. If she was to be single for the rest of her life, she needed to figure some things out. Like her future.

Over lunch, Simone's parents talked about their upcoming move to North Dakota.

"We're going to fly up next week for tests," Mom said. "When we get back, we'll work on closing up the house."

Simone set her fork on her plate. "What if I go with you?"

Her parents exchanged a glance.

Olivia's look was hopeful. "You'd do that?"

"I'm thinking about it," Simone answered.

Mom shook her head. "No, sweetie. I don't think that's a good idea. You have a job here and a life."

Simone huffed out a laugh. Quite a life she had. Her friends were involved in their coupled-up lives. Her job was boring and dead-end. The only bright spot was the challenge of preparing Gabe for his upcoming challenge. Except that he was kind of a jerk. Also looming was the offer from DavidJon.

Dad chimed in. "Simone, we don't know how long we'll be gone. It could be a few weeks, or it could be a few months. Your mom's right. You shouldn't drop everything to tag along with us."

"I wouldn't be tagging along. I could go and, oh, I don't know, prepare food so you wouldn't have to worry about meals. I could take care of laundry and things like that."

Mom's eyes filled with tears. "That's sweet, Simone. But no. You can't stay tied to us forever. It's time to cut those apron strings." She glanced at Simone's dad. "We've been meaning to talk to you about attending church in Main. You shouldn't be driving here every Sunday for church. You need to go to church in your own community and make connections there.”

Simone felt like the bottom just dropped and she was free-falling. Her parents didn’t want her to go with them. They would move to North Dakota and leave her behind. Just like Adam.

A sob worked its way up from her belly and stuck in her throat. Tears pushed their way out of her eyes.

“Oh, sweetie.” Mom’s voice was full of compassion as she got up from her seat and walked around the table to pull Simone into a hug. “It’ll be okay.”

Simone sobbed into her mother’s shoulder.

“Shh, Simone. Don’t cry.”

Olivia looked up at Simone, her face stricken. “But I want Sis to come with us.”

Simone’s mother grabbed a napkin off the table and wiped Simone’s face. She cupped Simone’s cheeks. “It’s time, Simone. Time to be on your own and figure your life out.”

Mom dropped her hands and looked down at Olivia. “You’ll be fine, O. I know you’ll miss your sister, but it’s only for a little while.”

Simone wanted to blurt, “What if Olivia dies?” But she kept the words unspoken.

When they said their goodbyes, her dad held her extra tight.

“I’m not sure if we’ll be back next Sunday or not. You need to go to the church in Main where your friends go, okay?”

Simone nodded but wasn’t happy about her father’s instruction. Going to Main Community meant seeing all her friends with their husbands, fiancés, and significant others. Going there was like wearing a sign that read: Single forever! Dumped by her fiancé! Do not approach!

She reluctantly agreed and drove back to Main with a heavy heart.

~

The first thing Gabe did Sunday morning was peek into his sister's room to make sure she was okay. Her breathing seemed normal, so he tiptoed closer to watch her sleeping form. The labor pains she'd had last night scared them.

Thankfully the twins slept through all the commotion, blissfully unaware of the drama. Satisfied Grace seemed to be okay, he backed out of her room and smack dab into his mom.

"You scared me," Mom whispered as Gabe closed Grace's bedroom door. "How's she doing?"

"She's sleeping. Seems to be okay," Gabe responded in a hushed tone.

They tread quietly down the hall and into the kitchen.

"Coffee?" Mom asked, holding up the pot.

"Always," Gabe answered. He rubbed the stubble on his cheeks with a weary sigh. "That was way too much like something I'd face at work."

Mom poured him a steaming cup of brew. "How is work going?"

Gabe shrugged. "Okay, I guess. I need to figure some things out."

"Such as?"

"My captain wants me to test for the next level." How to explain to his mom the lethargy he'd felt since Tiffany's betrayal? He hadn't cared about getting ahead or being promoted. The 9/11 challenge was the only thing that had sparked his interest since then. He hoped being part of the event would reignite his love for his job.

His mom sat at the table. Gabe sat across from her.

"Why did you apply for the job in South Carolina if there's a chance to move up where you're at?" Mom regarded him over the rim of her cup.

Gabe shrugged. "Something different, I guess."

"Gabriel Bruce, that's a ridiculous answer."

He set his cup on the table and ran a finger around the rim. "I'm kinda glad I didn't get the job. I'd be too far away from you, Dad, and Grace. Especially now."

Mom reached across the table and laid a hand on his forearm. "Gabe, honey. You have to live your life. If getting a new job someplace else is the best thing for you, I say go for it."

Gabe looked into his mother's eyes. "Really?"

Mom released her grasp and wrapped her hands around her mug. "Your dad told me about Tiffany." She clucked her tongue. "I'm so sorry, honey. You know we would have accepted her and the baby, if that's what you wanted."

The familiar dual pang of pain and guilt hit him in the gut. His family would have accepted her. That's what he loved about them. When Grace brought Demarcus home to meet them, they hadn't batted an eye. They'd embraced him and only asked that he love Grace and take care of her. They would have grown to love Tiffany, too. But that ship had sailed.

"Let's talk about something else," Mom said. "Tell me about Simone."

Gabe's heart stopped, skipped a beat, and started again. "What about her?" He hid his face behind his mug, taking several mouth-scalding sips.

Mom smiled knowingly. "I saw the way you looked at her."

"We're friends, Mom."

Mom scraped her chair back and stood. "You keep telling yourself that, Son. But I don't for one moment believe it."

Gabe frowned, remembering his last conversation with Simone as she practically sprinted to her car yesterday.

He pulled his phone toward him to check for any texts from her. He scrolled back through their texts and saw the one he hadn't been able to finish because Grace's cries for help had interrupted what he'd planned to say.

"Because friends don't let friends." What had he meant to say? Friends don't let friends stay mad? Friends don't let friends steal all the attention?

"I'm going to go get ready for church," Gabe said, pushing back from the table.

As he turned to leave, his mom said, "Why don't you invite Simone over for dinner today?"

Gabe sent his mom a rueful smile. "I would, but she spends Sundays with her family. In Salem."

"All day?"

"She has dinner or something with her girlfriends when she gets back."

His mom laughed. "For someone who's just a friend, you seem to know a lot about her schedule."

Gabe was saved from answering by the arrival of Mercy and Hope.

"Uncle Gabe," they exclaimed, jumping up with arms raised. "Pick me up!"

He grabbed a girl in each arm and swung them

around while they squealed.

"Quiet, girls, or you'll wake your mom," His mom warned.

Gabe let them slide down his legs to the floor. "I guess we'll take this up later. Outside." He leaned down to ruffle the girls' hair. As he did, he remembered how Simone had stared at the girls yesterday. They shared the same mocha-colored skin and light eyes. If they had kids, what would they look like?

Stop, he told himself. Friends don't let friends think about having kids together.

Chapter 22

Church that morning started with a rousing set of worship songs. Gabe waved to Simone's friend, Mariah, and her fiancée. What was his name again? Something with an E. He shrugged.

See Mom, I don't know everything about my friend.

Pastor Roy's sermon was on the prodigal son from Luke 15. Gabe felt every heartbeat in his head as the pastor spoke. He tied in the verse from 2 Timothy that said to 'flee youthful lusts.' He could have prevented a lot of misery in his life and in Tiffany's if he'd fled youthful lusts.

Pastor Roy reminded the congregation that just as the prodigal's father showed mercy and forgiveness, God also shows mercy and forgiveness. All He asks is repentance.

Gabe bowed his head during the closing prayer and thanked God for forgiveness for the way he'd treated Tiffany and for the life she'd taken.

He walked out of the church feeling like he'd just slipped off the fifty-pound backpack he'd worn during their run in the Basket Slough.

The urge to talk to Simone had him grabbing his phone. He started a text, but his parents pulled him away, anxious to return home and check on Grace. After helping get the twins into their car seats, Gabe had no time to return to his phone. Sitting between the girls on the drive home meant entertaining them with silly songs and made-up stories.

At the house, his mom scurried into Grace's room. Gabe overheard their voices discussing Grace's condition. She was stable. For now. The ER doctor said Saturday's excitement had been too much. From now on, she had to stay in a prone position and avoid over-stimulation.

Toward the afternoon, Gabe and his dad relaxed on the back porch and watched clouds gather over the hills separating Main from the coast.

"We may have some rain later," Dad commented.

"You don't sound worried." Unexpected rain could sometimes mean disaster for the seed farm.

"It might set us back a bit."

"The rain could help with the wildfires further east," Gabe said. He'd seen the reports about fires blazing in the forest toward Sisters, Oregon. He remembered the devastating effects of the Santiam Fire in 2020 that blew into Main. The sky over his parents' farm was angry crimson for days. People lost their homes, their livelihoods, and their lives. Gabe and his fellow firefighters had been on the front lines of that blaze.

Gabe's dad's face wore lines of worry. "Let's hope the rain blows that direction."

"And the fire stays that direction too." Gabe's buddies might be preparing to be deployed while he sat in comfort on his parents' back porch. Maybe he should chuck the idea of the 9/11 challenge and head back to

Portland. His mom might be able to get help from some women in the church so she could be with Dad in the fields.

His leg bounced up and down as he considered his options.

Dad's voice interrupted his thoughts. "What are you thinking?"

Gabe swept a hand through his hair. "Whether I should go back to Portland to be with my company. In case the wildfires spread."

Dad clapped him on the shoulder. "You do what you have to, Son. We'll figure things out here."

"I'll text my captain and see what he says."

"I don't say this often enough, Gabe, but I'm proud of you. You've made some mistakes, but you were prepared to man up with Tiffany. You admitted your mistake and took responsibility for your sin. Mom and I couldn't be prouder."

Gabe's eyes filled with tears. He blinked them back and spoke over the thickness in his throat. "Thanks, Dad."

Dad got to his feet. "I'm gonna go in the house now before we turn into blubbering idiots."

Gabe watched his dad's back until he closed the door behind him. He hoped to be half the man his dad was someday. To have the love of a good woman like his mom for over twenty years. How long had his parents been married, anyway? He tried to do the math and gave up.

Gabe sent a quick text to Captain Wells. He scrolled to the texts with Simone and considered his words, settling on something innocuous.

Gabe: Hope your day is going well. See you

tomorrow.

He waited for the bubbles showing she was composing an answer, but his phone screen stayed static.

~

Simone's phone lit up with a text on her way from her parents' house to Main. She'd look at it once she arrived at Cookie's Cafe for dinner with Mariah and Lizzy. Although the last thing she wanted was to act normal with her friends. She'd much prefer to crawl into bed and pull the covers over her head.

Her folks' announcement about moving left her rudderless. Her mom's intent had been to set her free. Wasn't that what she wanted? To be able to travel without guilt? To move someplace else without having to consider her parents?

Simone kept an eye on her speed in case Carl the Cop was patrolling the area. After her abrupt turn down of his dates, he might not be as lenient this time if she got pulled over.

She pulled into the cafe parking lot and turned off the ignition. Her cell phone showed a text from Gabe.

Gabe: Hope your day is going well. See you tomorrow.

Nope, her day wasn't going well. It was a hot mess. She was a hot mess. She shoved the phone in her purse.

Lizzy was just pulling up as Simone got out of the car.

"Look at you," Simone exclaimed. "You're really starting to show."

Lizzy grinned and stroked her growing belly. "He's an active one, that's for sure."

They walked into Cookie's Cafe arm in arm.

Simone shoved down the feelings of jealousy that threatened to sour her friend's joy.

Lizzy deserved to be happy after all she'd been though. Unexpected pregnancy at sixteen. Being a struggling single mom. Dealing with Abby's dad after a ten-year absence. Now she had a great husband in Roman and a new little one on the way.

Simone hated herself for feeling jealous. She'd been the one to get engaged while Lizzy and Roman were still trying to figure things out. Simone had more in common with Mariah, whose fiancé dumped her too. But even Simone's former enemy, Mean Girl Mariah was now a nicer, gentler version of herself. And was engaged to the church's youth pastor.

Odd man out. That was her. Simone's feet dragged as Lizzy led her to a table on the back patio of the cafe.

"You beat us here, Mariah," Lizzy said.

"I wanted a little time alone," Mariah said with a smile. "Ethan is at my house with Jayden and the two kids I'm watching for Safe Families."

"How's that going?" Lizzy asked while she and Simone took their seats.

Simone only half-listened while Mariah launched into a description of her two latest assignments. Mariah had jumped into this program of helping people out of difficult situations by watching their kids so they could get on their feet.

While Simone admired Mariah for doing it, she'd have rather stuck a pencil in her eye than listen to Mariah enthuse about how cute the kids were.

When Mariah stopped talking, Simone looked up from staring at her lap to find her two friends exchanging a glance.

"What?" Simone asked.

Lizzy spoke first. "We are going to have an intervention." Her words dropped on the table like a ten-pound medicine ball.

Mariah nodded. "That's right."

"An intervention? For me?" Simone drew back and readied herself to dash from the table.

Lizzy laid a hand on Simone's shoulder. "Before you get all huffy, Mariah and I want to say we love you. But since that guy whose name we won't mention left, you've become someone we don't recognize."

"Yeah, Simone. You're starting to act like I used to," Mariah added.

Simone pressed her lips together to keep from spewing words that might not be Christ-like.

"You've lost yourself. You get mad way too easy and you're starting to sound bitter."

"I am not," Simone protested. But the truth of Lizzy's words hurt like a bruise.

"Yes, you are. I know more than anyone how bitterness can destroy you," Mariah added.

Lizzy patted Simone's shoulder. "Talk to us, girlfriend. What's going on? We want to know everything."

Simone took a deep breath and dove into a ten-minute discourse on how awful her life was. Her parents were moving out of state, Olivia had cancer, she had a job offer from an old college friend in Beaverton, and most of all there was the problem of Gabe. She left out the kissing part.

"He wants to be friends, which I guess is fine . . ." Simone's voice trailed off.

"But you want more," Lizzy said with a knowing

smile.

"I don't know what I want." That part was true. Did she want to relocate to Beaverton where she didn't know anyone except DavidJon? Or should she quit her job and fly to Spain for the Camino de Santiago? Add in the growing attraction to Mr. Glory Hog. She let her head drop into her hands.

Mariah took a sip of her diet soda. "Have you prayed about this, Simone?"

Simone gulped. Count on Mariah to get straight to the heart. "Maybe. Not really." Sure, she'd whispered a few words of prayer for Olivia, but not for herself. Granny's conversation poked a bony finger in her heart.

"That's your problem. The main thing I've learned since becoming a Christian is that prayer is super important." Mariah stabbed the table with one long, pink-tipped finger.

Lizzy nodded. "It's true. You've seen my life and how crazy it's been. But since you invited me to church, God has always pulled me through every situation."

Simone had to agree. Lizzy's life had been roller-coaster crazy. Now she had everything she wanted. This time was supposed to be Simone's. Instead, she had to watch from the sidelines as her two besties found their true love.

"You're doing it again," Lizzy said. "I know you better than anyone and I can see the wheels turning."

Simone clenched her teeth, waiting for the rest of Lizzy's pronouncement.

"Your time will come, Simone. Whether it's with Gabe or someone else, God has someone picked out just for you. The other decisions are just that.

Decisions. There's no right or wrong way to go. God is able to bring your man to you, if that's what you want, whether you're in North Dakota, Beaverton, Spain, or right here in Main."

Mariah had to add her two cents. "In the meantime, you need to take a good, hard look at yourself and decide what kind of person you're going to be. Bitter or better?"

Simone choked out a laugh. "That's such a cliche."

Mariah joined her with a chuckle. "It's the best I could come up with on short notice."

Simone let out a deep sigh. "Okay, girls. Here's what I promise to do. Number one, stop being jealous of you two. Number two, spend more quality time praying about what I should do. Number three—"

"Give the guy a chance," said Mariah and Lizzy at the same time.

Chapter 23

Monday morning dawned with a blood-red sky. Gabe smelled the familiar scent of burning forest and yearned to be on the front lines of the fire.

He found his dad in the kitchen, pouring coffee into a Yeti mug.

"I'm going to head out and make sure the fire break I made last year is still intact. You coming?"

"Let me get some java first. I'll follow you out there in my pickup." Gabe snagged a mug from the dish drainer and poured himself a cup.

Dad nodded and headed out the door. Gabe heard his mom in the twin's bedroom, helping them get dressed for the day.

Gabe's phone rang. When he pulled out of his pocket, the caller ID said, "Main Fire Department."

"This is Gabe."

"Gabe, this is Nicolas. Is this too early to call?"

"Nope. Just having my first shot of caffeine." Gabe cradled the phone in his hand and put it on speaker.

"This is out of the blue, and I understand if you say no, but one of our guys took a job in Eugene. Would you be interested in working here?" Nicolas's voice sounded hopeful.

"Working at the Fire Department? Here in Main?"

"I'm being promoted to Captain and the guy who left was a lieutenant. I don't have anyone who's tested up yet. I figured you'd be able to slide right in, test up, and be a part of my team."

Gabe whistled. This was unexpected.

Nicolas continued. "I know it isn't as exciting as Portland. But you'd be surprised at the good we do here in Main, besides fighting fires."

Nicolas was doing his best to sell Gabe on the idea. "I know you need to think about it, Gabe. I hope you will. Think about it, that is."

"Sure. Okay. When do you need an answer?"

"How about in a week?"

Gabe promised to let Nicolas know by the following Monday. He disconnected and slumped back on the wooden kitchen chair. He'd think about the advantages and disadvantages of Nicolas's offer later. Right now, his dad needed him, and the afternoon held the promise of another workout with the sadist masquerading as a personal trainer.

Gabe drove his pickup slowly along the east edge of his parents' property. Dad had cleared vegetation from a six-foot area along the perimeter to slow down or stop the spread of a wildfire. Gabe knew sometimes fire breaks didn't work. The changing direction of the wind could throw sparks that might land in a dry area and create a new blaze.

In September of 2020, dry conditions and unusually high winds contributed to multiple fires throughout the state of Oregon. Despite the best efforts of their residents to create a buffer between their homes and the fires, over forty thousand people were evacuated from their homes and over a million acres were destroyed.

Gabe couldn't bear to think of his dad's livelihood being destroyed because of someone's carelessness. He didn't know about other states, but in Oregon, over ninety percent of wildfires are caused by humans.

He caught up with his dad after an hour of keeping his speedometer at five miles per hour or less. Throwing the truck in park, he got out and waited for his dad to climb down from the tractor.

"How's it looking over there?" Dad asked.

"Looks good."

They both gazed into the distance to the east where the sky was dark with smoke. Small bits of ash like black snow filtered down and landed on their shoulders.

"The air quality is bad," Dad said, squinting up.

Gabe felt the familiar tickle in his throat from the smoke. What were his guys doing right now? Were they on their way south to battle the red beast? What was he doing here, pretending to help his dad and flirting with Simone? He should be with his company.

"I'm going to take another trip around the property with the tractor. Why don't you go on back to the house and check on Mom and the girls." Dad pulled his John Deere hat off, rubbed his head, and jammed it back on his head.

"Make sure their go-bags are at the ready."

Worry lines around his dad's mouth formed deep vees. "Okay, Dad."

His dad climbed back onto the tractor and took a long drink from his Yeti mug. Soon the growl of the tractor grew faint as his dad headed away.

Gabe got back into his truck and grabbed his cell phone. He did a quick search for updates on the fire burning to the east. The fire was fifty percent contained. Satisfied, he headed into the house.

"What are you doing back so soon?" Mom greeted him at the back door.

"Dad's worried about the fire. But I think it's far enough away and enough contained that it won't reach us. Still, he told me to make sure your go-bags are packed and ready."

Mom bit her lip and frowned. "If he's that concerned . . ."

Gabe pulled her into a hug. "He's being cautious, that's all. It'll be fine."

From what he'd read online, they had no reason to worry. The wildfire was ninety miles away and rapidly coming under control. The wind was blowing due west, bringing the soot and smoke their way, but not the blaze.

Gabe wished he could erase the worried lines from his mother's face. She had a lot on her plate. Caring for the twins, guilty over not being out with Dad in the field, concern for Grace and her baby. Adulting was hard.

Gabe took a moment to check on his sister. He found her napping in one of the recliners in the living room. For once, her girls were playing quietly with Legos on the floor. He backed out of the room without being noticed.

Since his dad didn't need him, Gabe might as well change and head to the gym. His pulse quickened at the thought of seeing Simone. He should never have suggested they be 'just friends.' *Grave tactical error, Harrison.*

Time to remedy that mistake. If he took Nicolas up

on his offer, Gabe would stay here in Main and pursue a relationship with Simone.

Unless she took the job in Beaverton.

The thought drew him up short.

~

Simone scratched her idea of having Gabe do the Basket Slough run again today. The smoky air was sharp in her lungs. It wouldn't be wise to exercise outside with the smoke thickening the atmosphere.

Simone made her usual tour through the large equipment room to ensure people used the weight machines properly to avoid injury. Most of the older folks appreciated her help. It was the young macho guys who resented her correction.

Simone spied Nicolas, working out on the leg machine. She walked over to greet him.

"Hi. We met Saturday at Grace's house."

Nicolas let the weights drop with a thunk. "Oh, hey. Simone, right?"

"Yes. Do you come here often?" Simone's hand flew to her mouth. "Oh, my gosh. That sounded like a pickup line. Which it wasn't. I meant I haven't seen you here before." Simone resisted the urge to fan her rapidly heating cheeks.

Nicolas had the grace to laugh it off. "Not to worry. I usually come super early, before work. Besides, I wouldn't think you'd be flirting with me since I'm married and you're with Gabe."

Simone shook her head. "Gabe and I, we're just friends."

Nicolas pinned her with a look. "You might want to check. I noticed how Gabe looked at you."

Simone saw the man himself push through the door

of the gym. She spun on her heels. "I have to go."

She dashed up the stairs to the second floor to check on the Pilates class. The music helped drown out the beating of her heart. When she was able to catch her breath, Simone crept down the stairs and checked to see if Gabe or Nicolas were in sight.

When she was sure the coast was clear, Simone stepped down the last couple of stairs.

"There you are." Mariah's voice made her jump. "I've been looking all over for you."

"What are you doing here?" Simone eyed Mariah up and down. She wore a pair of flowered leggings and a snug top accentuating her lithe figure.

Mariah sent her a smug smile. "I came to work out, of course. And to check out your client. You know, your friend."

Simone looked over Mariah's shoulder to see her boss, Carson, Gabe, and his friend Nicolas stepping out of the gym office. She grabbed Mariah's arm and yanked her to the other side of the room.

"Shh," she cautioned. "There he is."

Mariah turned her body to look toward the men. "He's cute. Explain to me again why you—"

"There's something I didn't tell you and Lizzy," Simone swung Mariah around so her back faced the guys. "He kissed me."

Mariah's squeal echoed off the gym ceiling. "How could you have forgotten such an important detail?"

"Shh! Good grief, Mariah." Simone's legs turned to mush when Gabe broke away from the two men and strode across the room toward them.

"Looks like you're having a better conversation over here than I was," Gabe said. To Mariah, he said,

"Nice to see you again. You go to my parents' church."

Mariah held out a manicured hand for Gabe to shake. "Yes, I do. My fiancé is the youth pastor."

"That's cool."

The conversation stuttered to a halt. Mariah slid her eyes from Simone to Gabe and back. "Well, I better get over to the treadmill. Bye." She waggled her fingers in Simone's direction with another knowing smile.

"Are you ready to work out?" Simone asked, hoping to discharge the emotional tension left by her friend.

"Can I make a suggestion?"

Simone regarded him with her mouth pulled to one side. "Okay."

"Can we do our workout on the beach? The air is clear there and running on the sand might be good. I'll even wear that darn backpack if you want."

Simone took several seconds to think. "Sure. Let's do it."

A change of scenery might be good for her. The beach was her happy place.

"I'll drive," Gabe said.

Simone sent him the stink-eye. "Why?"

"Because I'm driving, that's why."

"Fine," Simone huffed. Just wait 'til they got to the beach. Then she'd show him who was boss.

Chapter 24

On the short drive to the ocean, Gabe talked about the fires burning to the east. Simone remembered the devastation and losses from the fires a few years ago. One of her coworker's family friends lost their home and one of their pets. Heartbreaking.

"How do you deal with all the destruction?" Simone asked. "Does it affect you after you finish your shift?"

Gabe's jaw tightened. "Sometimes it does, yeah. It helps to have a good support system."

"And do you? Have a good support system?"

Gabe's knuckles turned white as he gripped the steering wheel. "I used to."

Simone figured he must be talking about his ex, Tiffany. Time to change the subject. "How's your sister?"

Gabe exhaled with a whoosh. "Much better. That was scary, her having labor pains. The doc gave her a stern lecture about overdoing her activity."

"I can imagine. I'm glad she's okay."

The conversation lagged as they pulled into the parking lot of the beach access in Newport.

"Are you ready to work, Glory?" Simone sent him a wicked grin.

Simone's face grew warm as Gabe stared at her mouth. Her grin faded. Why did he have to have that effect on her? Not fair. He was leaving at the end of the month. Best for her to keep her heart intact.

They clambered out of Gabe's pickup and walked to the edge of the asphalt.

"Let's warm up and then we'll do a timed run."

Simone led Gabe through some stretches before setting the timer on her smart watch. She pointed to where the beach ended in a rocky outcropping. "Let's jog to there and sprint back."

She led him in an easy pace on the soft sand. "Try to keep up," she said with a smile.

Gabe laughed. "As if."

Gabe kept pace as Simone sped up ever-so-slightly. She breathed in the briny scent of decaying seaweed mixed with sunscreen oozing off the sunbathers they passed. They dodged children chasing the waves and wet dogs prancing in the shallow water.

"Did I tell you I got a call from Nicolas?" Gabe asked, his breath coming in short puffs.

"Nicolas from the fire department? Nope."

"He offered me," huff, "a job." More huffing.

Simone digested this. If Gabe decided to stay in Main, would that influence her decision to move to Beaverton and work with DavidJon?

"Same thing you're doing now?" Simone asked.

"Yeah. But a promotion."

Simone sent him a sideways glance. "Is that what you want?"

They reached the pile of rocks. Simone didn't wait for Gabe's answer. She whirled around and sprinted back the way they'd come. A quick glance over her shoulder showed Gabe was a few steps behind her.

Confusion dogged her steps as she fought the loose sand shifting under her Hokas. What if Gabe didn't go back to Portland? What would it be like to see him around town or at the gym? Maybe it would be best for her to take the job in Beaverton after all.

She glanced over her shoulder to see if Gabe was still behind her. Her heart stopped when she spied him writhing on the ground several yards away.

"Oh my gosh! What happened?"

~

Gabe's calf was as hard as concrete. Simone's shadow covered him.

"What happened?"

He could only grind out one word. "Cramp." He grabbed his calf with both hands, willing the muscles to relax. He groaned out loud, an animal-like sound.

Simone bent over him and pushed his hands away. Using her own hands, she massaged his leg.

"Try to relax."

Gabe spoke through clenched teeth. "I am relaxing."

Simone attempted to pull his leg straight. "No, you aren't."

When the cramp eased, Gabe hoped she would keep massaging his calf. Her hands were strong, yet gentle. When his breathing returned to normal, Gabe pushed himself to a sitting position.

"Thanks."

Simone sat back on her haunches. "How much water have you been drinking?"

Gabe shrugged. "I dunno."

"Clearly not enough." Simone sent him a disgusted

look. "You've been working in the sun with your dad, right?" She didn't wait for his response. "Then you come to the gym and work out. Your body needs potassium. Electrolytes. The lactic acid buildup in your muscles—"

Gabe grabbed Simone's hand. "I get it. Drink more water. Add some salt to my diet. Have a sports drink."

Simone pulled her hand from his grasp. "Sheesh. You don't have to get all huffy." She rose in one graceful movement. "Think you can get yourself up, Glory?"

Gabe felt two inches tall. He was being schooled by a girl. Woman. Whatever. He struggled to his feet and took a couple of limping steps. Simone watched him with concern in her eyes.

"Guess I won't be sprinting back with you."

"Some people will do anything to get out of running." A smile worked its way up to her mouth.

Gabe shrugged. "It worked, didn't it?"

Gabe set a slow pace back to where they'd begun. His leg would be sore for a couple of days, that he was sure of. Simone was right, though. He'd paid little attention to his water intake.

"Will you be okay to drive back?" Simone asked when they reached his truck.

"I'd have to be dead to let someone else drive my pickup," Gabe said, hitting the remote to unlock the doors. "Speaking of dead, the motorcycle guy is super lucky to be alive. Did you know that CPR is only successful about ten percent of the time?"

Simone climbed into the cab of his pickup. "I've heard that. But I'd say he's blessed, not lucky."

Gabe stuck his key into the ignition. "True that."

They drove back to the gym in silence. When he pulled into the parking lot, Simone asked, "Are you coming in?"

"Yeah, I thought I'd say hello to Carson. We had plans to get together for a couple of brews later."

Gabe opened the door to Gym Time to allow Simone to pass. Her friend, Mariah, was standing in the door to Carson's office, talking with him. She waved at the two of them.

Gabe limped over to them, Simone on his heels. Before he could greet them, a familiar voice shrilled behind him.

"I thought I'd find you here."

Gabe swung around. "Tiffany. What are you doing here?"

~

Simone's muscles tensed as her eyes landed on the woman approaching Gabe. His ex-girlfriend. Tiffany slinked forward, her body clad in a pair of knee-high leather boots and a skirt so short it could easily be mistaken for a handkerchief. Her top hung off one shoulder, revealing a bright pink bra strap that seemed to taunt Simone's tidy whiteys. A bead of sweat dripped down Simone's spine, emphasizing every grain of sand on her skin. How could she ever compete with this? Tiffany looked effortlessly put together, more than Mariah ever had. But as Simone studied her closer, she noticed the brittleness in Tiffany's features, a hint of insecurity beneath her perfectly styled exterior. Simone felt a rush of relief. Maybe she didn't have to compete after all.

Tiffany laid French-tipped fingers on Gabe's arm. "You were always a gym rat. I'm glad I found you here.

We need to talk."

Simone watched Gabe's features harden. "I have nothing to say to you."

Tiffany pouted. "Gabe, honey, I can't stand the way we left things."

"The way *you* left things," Gabe said, shaking her hand off.

Mariah stepped forward into Tiffany's personal space. "What Gabe is saying is you need to leave."

Tiffany glared at Mariah. "Who are you?"

Simone watched Mariah morph into Mean Girl Mariah. She took a step back to get out of Mariah's line of fire.

Mariah moved a bit closer to Tiffany. "I'm one of Gabe's friends. His real friends."

Mariah made a sweeping motion with her arm. "As you might have noticed, this is a gym." She swept her gaze up and down the other woman. "You are clearly not dressed to work out." Mariah pointed to the door. "The exit is that way."

Tiffany exhaled with a little squeak. "Gabe, honey, are you going to let her talk to me like that?"

Gabe shrugged.

"Huh. Fine. I'll wait for you outside." Tiffany fluffed her blonde hair and stomped to the exit.

Simone gave a low whistle. "Wow. I haven't seen that side of you in a long time."

Mariah's grin was wolfish. "I know, right? I'm sure I'm going to have to repent later. But, boy did that feel good." She rubbed her crossed arms.

"Have you thought of a career as a bouncer?" Carson asked.

Everyone cracked up, including the oldsters who'd

stopped their workouts to watch the drama. A few of the men hooted and clapped.

Mariah's face turned red. "I better get home. I'm sure Ethan will have heard about this before I pull up in front of my house." She sent a smile to Gabe. "Small towns."

Gabe nodded. "You got that right."

"I'm gonna go home and shower," Simone said. "You should go home, too, and put some heat on that cramp." She followed Mariah out the exit.

"You didn't have to do that," Simone said, pointing back toward the gym.

Mariah flipped her hair over one shoulder. "I know. But I couldn't resist. She looked toxic. We can't have that drama around your guy."

"He isn't my guy," Simone said, narrowing her eyes.

Mariah laughed as she climbed into her Beemer. "Yeah, but you'd like him to be." She closed the car door before Simone could respond.

Chapter 25

Simone relished the piercing spray of hot water, sluicing off the sand and ocean mist from her skin. She'd washed her hair and used a wide-toothed comb, dividing her messy locks into sections. Once the tangles were out, she wrapped her head in a satin scarf. She'd deal with the flat iron tomorrow.

Her phone pinged with an incoming text.

Gabe: When are you going up to Beaverton?

Simone: Tomorrow.

She'd had a long chat with her friend DavidJon. He'd practically promised her a percentage of the business if she'd accept his offer to come work for him.

"I'll be there Tuesday afternoon," she'd told him. Might as well get a feel for what his new boutique gym was all about.

Gabe: Want me to drive you? I have to go to Portland and talk to my supervisor.

Simone tapped her forefinger on the screen. Did she want to spend several hours with Gabe? Yes, she did. Was it a good idea? No.

Simone: Sure. What time?

Gabe: How's 1:00?

A tickle of nerves fluttered in her stomach. She sent Gabe a thumbs up emoji and fell back onto the bed with a smile. She raised the phone to her face and tapped out a response.

Simone: Friends don't let friends drive to Beaverton alone

Gabe responded with a laughing emoji.

~

Gabe stretched out on his bed with his hands under his head. What had possessed Tiffany to show up at Gym Time and try to talk? The only thing he could say to her would be, "I'm sorry. Now go away."

He at least owed her that. He tried to call her when he got back to his parents', but she didn't answer. Typical Tiffany. Passive aggressive to the extreme. What had he ever seen in her?

Lust. That was what he'd seen. He'd let his baser instincts possess him. Look how that turned out.

After several minutes of self-flagellation, Gabe forced his thoughts away from Tiffany and to God. Forgiveness was free and all Gabe had to do was receive it. Until he asked Tiffany for forgiveness, there would still be unfinished business between them.

He tried to call her again and got her voice mail. "Tiffany, this is Gabe. We should talk. Maybe tomorrow or Wednesday. Call me back, please."

Since that was now on hold, Gabe let his mind wander to Simone. They'd agreed to be friends, but after their kiss, that was all he could think about. Tomorrow, he'd have at least an hour drive to Beaverton, another forty-five minutes to his station, then back to Main. There'd be no kissing while he was driving, but maybe . . .

Slow down, G-man. This was a relationship he needed to take slowly. Not like with Tiffany. They'd gone from 'nice to meet you' to 'let's move in together' with barely a breath. Simone's faith wouldn't let her get intimate until marriage. Did he want to look that far ahead?

~

Simone dashed through the front door of her apartment at 12:45. One of her clients had kept her longer than she'd planned. Gabe said he'd be at her place at one o'clock and he'd be on time, as usual.

Giving up on the idea of a quick shower, she splashed on some deodorant, slid some pink lip gloss over her lips, and obsessed over what to wear. Would DavidJon expect her to show up in workout clothes? Or would it be better to wear something more professional? It wasn't a job interview. More of a discussion. He wanted her to join him, so really it was up to Simone to decide what she wanted.

The bed sagged under her weight as Simone considered her clothing options. Finally deciding on a pair of khaki shorts and a green tee, she fluffed her hair and slid on a pair of sandals.

The doorbell rang at exactly one. Simone grabbed her purse and swung open the door. Gabe looked good. Too good. He also wore shorts, showing off those to-die-for legs.

"Hi." Her voice was breathless as she pulled the door closed behind her.

"Hi, yourself. You look nice."

Nice. So innocuous. "Is that the best you could come up with, Glory?"

Gabe grinned down at her. "Now whose ego is on

full display?" He looked her up and down. "You look really nice."

Simone smiled despite herself. "C'mon, let's go." She strode to his pickup. Before she could reach for the door handle, Gabe grabbed it and swung it open.

"Allow me," he said with a gallant sweep of his arm.

Gabe pointed the truck toward Salem on Highway 22. Simone held her breath as they passed the place where the motorcyclist went down. Her mind returned to the panic she'd felt watching him fly off the road.

Simone twirled the promise ring around and around.

"You nervous?" Gabe asked, glancing at her hand.

"How can you tell?"

"When you're nervous or unsure you play with your ring. What's the significance of that, anyway?"

Simone stared down at the tiny diamond twinkling in the sunlight streaming through the windows. "It's a promise ring. Or a purity ring. My dad gave it to me when I turned sixteen. I made a promise to him I'd stay sexually pure until I got married."

"And have you?"

Simone sent him a hard look. "I'm still wearing the ring, aren't I?"

Gabe rubbed a spot on his chest. "Ouch. Point taken." After a moment, he said, "Are you nervous about this job interview?"

Simone stared at the passing landscape, considering how to answer. Groves of trees and sprawling farmhouses were separated by fields of grass, corn, and alfalfa.

"It isn't really an interview, per se. Basically, my friend wants me to come up and work with him in his new gym. I have to decide whether I want to."

"Do you? Want to?"

That was the million-dollar question. What did she want?

~

Gabe watched the play of emotions on Simone's face from his question.

He was in the same situation—limbo. His conversation with this captain might help clarify what to do. Should he go back to Portland and test up? Or apply for the position in Main and test up to lieutenant there?

If Simone decided to move to Beaverton, should he stay in Portland so he'd be close to her? Maybe see if there could be more to their relationship than just friends?

He must have made a sound of frustration, because Simone's head swiveled toward him.

"What are you thinking?" she asked.

"I'm thinking that today is a perfect day for a drive. And a perfect day to stop by Salt and Straw in Portland for some amazing ice cream."

Simone smiled and nodded. "I think that's a great idea." She reached for the button on his radio. "How about some road trip tunes?"

Gabe handed her his cell phone and the cord. "I have a great playlist for just this occasion."

Simone connected the phone and Gabe instructed her on where the playlist was.

"My car is so old I don't have any of this cool tech," Simone said.

Gabe raised his eyebrows. "Your car is very … orange."

"Don't be hating on Orange Crush. She's very dependable."

Gabe snickered. "You named your car Orange Crush?"

"Yes. What's the problem?"

"Do you always name your car?"

"You don't?"

"I'd have to give up my man card if I named my vehicle."

It was Simone's turn to laugh. "Not likely, Glory."

Gabe warmed to their exchange. It was a lot more fun exchanging barbs with Simone than he'd ever had with Tiffany. Speaking of, she still hadn't returned his call. He'd give her twenty-four more hours before he tried again. Her attempt to punish him by ghosting would not affect him this time.

Simone's voice broke into his thoughts. "Where'd you go?"

Gabe shifted on the seat, adjusting the seatbelt across his body. "Have you ever done something you regret?"

Simone huffed out a laugh. "All the time."

"Really? I thought you were like a super-Christian or something."

Gabe felt the heat of her glare from across the cab.

"Excuse me? Super-Christian? For your information, even Christians make mistakes. Surely, you've figured that out by now."

Gabe felt heat rising from his neck. "My bad. I didn't mean to get you all mad. What I meant was, I didn't think you'd have many regrets. You seem like you have it all together."

When Simone didn't answer, he hazarded a glance

at her face. A tear had gathered in the one eye he could see as she stared out the windshield.

Chapter 26

Gabe's words struck deep and reopened wounds she had been trying to heal. Since Adam walked out of her life, everything had fallen apart. Her once stable future was now in shambles. Just when she thought things couldn't get any worse, her sister's diagnosis came crashing down on her like a hundred-pound dumbbell. Each step she took felt like walking on shards of glass, constantly reminding her of the pain and uncertainty that consumed her every day.

"I don't have it all together," Simone whispered.

Gabe's hand engulfed hers. He squeezed gently. "I doubt any of us really have it all together. It's a huge facade."

Simone relaxed as the warmth from Gabe's hand spread comfort. She used her other hand to swipe at her tears. "Sorry. I don't usually get emotional. This thing with my sister has me torn up."

"I can relate." Gabe released her hand to reach for the volume control, turning down the music. "Family is super important to me. Although, I lost sight of that fact for a while."

"Tiffany?"

Gabe's mouth turned down. "Yeah. That was a

disaster. I wish I could go back and have a do-over." He glanced her way. "Know what I mean?"

Simone sighed. "Yup. I'd go back and rethink my relationship with Adam. There were signs. I just didn't want to see them."

Gabe smacked the steering wheel with one hand. "Let's make a pact. The past is in the past. Let's start fresh today. What do you think?"

"Do you mind if I quote a Scripture verse?"

"Go for it."

"Lamentations 3: 23 says that God's mercies are new every morning."

Gabe seemed to consider her words. "Sounds good. New every morning. I like it."

Gabe turned the volume back up and began to sing along with the Beach Boy's classic California Girls. Simone laughed at his off-key singing and joined him on the chorus.

Simone pointed ahead to a building tucked into a strip mall. "There it is. We can park here."

She fingered the promise ring as nerves settled into her stomach. She took a couple of calming breaths while Gabe parked his truck.

"Want me to go in with you?"

Simone bit her bottom lip. "Okay, I guess. Sure." She climbed out of the pickup and eyed the outside windows. DavidJon had painted his logo and the name on the windows.

Go Through It Fitness. Underneath were the smaller words, 'If you can't go over it or under it, go through it.' Next to the words was a character holding a dumbbell.

Simone pulled open the door and stepped into the

facility. Fifteen or so spin bikes were arranged in two rows. Further back on one side was a workout area with free weights and other miscellaneous equipment.

DavidJon appeared through a door marked 'Office.'

"Shut the front door!" he exclaimed. "Look who just walked in." He strode over and engulfed Simone in a hug.

DavidJon pulled back and examined Simone from head to toe. "You look amazing."

"And you haven't changed a bit," Simone said with a smile.

DavidJon stuck out a hand toward Gabe. "DavidJon McFarland."

The men shook hands while Simone crossed her arms over her middle. She looked around the gym with an appraising eye. A large screen television hung on the wall in front of the spin bikes. Several motivational posters and sayings graced the red and black walls. A cubby for shoes and gym bags sat inside the front door.

"Come on back to the office," DavidJon said. "We can talk there."

Simone sent Gabe a questioning look.

"I'll go find some coffee or something," Gabe said, pointing a thumb over his shoulder.

"Thanks," Simone said. "Give us about an hour."

"Will do." Gabe headed out the door.

"That your boyfriend?" DavidJon asked.

Simone huffed out a laugh. "Not even. It's a long story but we're just friends."

DavidJon's smile was white against his ebony skin. "Sure, honey. Keep telling yourself that."

Simone rolled her eyes. "Let's talk about business, okay?"

DavidJon shrugged. "Whatever. By the way, Nicole says hi."

"Tell your wife I'm sorry I missed her."

DavidJon led Simone into his office. The décor was organized chaos. A three-drawer filing cabinet sat in one corner with the top drawer pulled out. On top were several bottles of water, some half-drunk and others empty. DavidJon's desk held an array of awards and miscellaneous scraps of paper. His laptop sat open on one corner.

"I'm so glad you're here," DavidJon said. "I plan to open in about three and a half weeks."

"That soon?" Panic pressed on her chest.

"Let me tell you about my business model."

DavidJon spent the next twenty minutes explaining his business plan.

"I expect to cater to an elite group of clients willing to pay top dollar for small group coaching. Class sizes will be limited to six people and spin classes to ten. I'll give you fifty percent of any personal coaching clients you bring in. You'll need to schedule them around the classes."

Simone's head spun as her friend extolled the benefits he offered to his clients. The salary he offered was slightly higher than what she currently made at Gym Time and she'd have the freedom to work one-on-one with people. Her favorites were the men and women over sixty who wanted to get back into shape or stay in shape as they aged.

"I can't offer health benefits right now. But once I really get rolling, I can add that."

"Sounds like an amazing opportunity."

"But?" DavidJon held up his hands, palms up.

Simone exhaled. "But I really need some time to think about it. I'd have to give notice at Gym Time, terminate my apartment lease, and find a place to live up here. It's a lot."

"I get it." DavidJon grimaced. "But I need an answer soon, Simone. If you say no, I've got to find someone else. I hope you understand."

"Sure." She rubbed sweaty palms down the legs of her shorts. "How about I give you an answer this weekend?"

DavidJon grinned. "As long as it's yes." He pushed himself to his feet. "What's the story with your guy?"

"Who, Gabe? I'm training him for the 9/11 Memorial Stair Challenge. He's a firefighter."

DavidJon's eyebrows rose. "No kidding? How's he doing?"

"Pretty good. Next week I'm going to have him in full uniform, tanks and all, on the stair machine."

"Good job. Lots of squats?"

"Oh, yeah. Squats, sprints, weights. I remember everything we were taught. I think he'll do fine."

DavidJon came around the desk and hugged her. "You're the best, Simone. That's why I want you here."

Simone's heart warmed. She needed his words of affirmation. Her primary love language.

"Thanks, DavidJon. I really appreciate your offer and I promise to think about it."

Simone found Gabe pacing back and forth in front of the building with his phone pressed against his ear.

"Yes, Tiffany," she heard him say.

Chapter 27

Gabe was relieved to talk to Tiffany. He wished the conversation went better and in person. But she wanted answers over the phone.

Tiffany tried crying to get his sympathy, then anger.

"I don't want to get back together with you," Gabe said for the third time. "I only wanted to let you know how sorry I am things turned out the way they did."

"But, Gabriel, baby, I still love you."

Gabe's grip on the phone tightened. "I'm sorry, Tiffany. It isn't going to work. We are over."

"It's about that girl, isn't it? The dark-skinned one in the gym."

Gabe blew out a breath. It *was* about Simone. But he wouldn't let his ex know that. "No, Tiff. It's about me telling you I'm sorry I put you in a bad situation. Please forgive me and let's both move on."

"Can I at least call you sometime?"

"Sure. Yes." Maybe.

Gabe spied Simone leaving the gym owned by her friend. "I gotta go." He disconnected before Tiffany could respond.

"Everything okay?" Simone asked.

"Awesome," Gabe answered with a frown. "Come

on, let's go." He spun toward the parking lot and strode to his pickup.

He opened the passenger door and waited for Simone to climb in. Walking slowly around the back of the truck, he willed his irritation to subside. He sucked in a breath and blew it out through pursed lips.

"Where to?" Simone asked as he clambered into the truck.

"I thought we could stop by my station real quick, then go get that ice cream I promised you."

Simone smiled. "Sounds good."

Gabe stayed silent on the way to his firehouse. What would his captain have to say? If he was even there. He and the men could have been called to the wildfires burning near Main, leaving a skeleton crew to manage any local issues. In a way, he'd be relieved if he didn't have to have any more difficult conversations today.

Glancing over at Simone, he asked, "Good talk with your friend?"

Simone's hand moved to her purity ring. "Yeah. I told DavidJon I'd let him know by this weekend if I'm going to take his offer."

"Did you and he, you know, date?" Gabe held his breath, waiting for her answer.

Simone burst out a laugh. "Me and DavidJon? Heck no. He's been married for, like, forever." She sent him a sideways glance. "Jealous, Glory?"

He was, but there was no way he'd admit it. Her friend DavidJon was tall, slim, and very buff.

"Ah, no. I'm concerned for you, that's all. I mean, if you did take the job, it wouldn't be good to date your boss." Lame, lame, lame. *You've lost your game, son.*

Simone put a hand over her mouth and laughed. "Sure. Whatever you say." Her laughter continued until they pulled up to Station House No. 3

~

Simone opted to wait in the pickup while Gabe went into the station.

"Captain Wells is out today," he was told. As was most of his company. Gabe left a message for his boss to call him and headed back to the truck.

"Ready for that ice cream?" he asked.

Simone looked up from her phone. "Always."

Gabe fastened his seat belt and started the truck.

"Did you know Salt and Straw was started by two cousins?" Gabe asked.

"And they had never made ice cream before. Cool story."

"They have a cult following, you know."

Simone nodded. "When I was going to college, we went there a lot."

Gabe circled the block until he found a parking spot. "Do you mind a short walk?"

"Not at all. I'll need to work off all that fatty goodness that's coming my way."

They strolled down the street. Gabe took in the fluffy clouds floating the blue sky overhead. Oregon summers were the best. He tolerated the rainy winters, but always waited anxiously for that first day of mild Spring weather. Without conscious thought, he grabbed Simone's hand. His heart quickened when she didn't pull away.

Swinging their arms between them, he asked, "Any idea what flavors you're going to get?"

"Oh, probably my usual. Mint chip and chocolate."

Gabe gave a fake gasp. "No, you aren't. It's time to try something new. If I'm paying, and I am, you are not allowed to get your usual."

Simone tugged at her hand, but Gabe didn't release his grip.

"Sorry, Simone, not gonna happen."

They reached the store, and Gabe used his other hand to open the door. The smell of ice cream and freshly made waffle cones filled the small space. Gabe inhaled.

"Yum."

Gabe gave Simone a gentle shove toward the tables on the other side of where the ice cream was on display. "You go find us a table. I'm going to order for you."

Simone opened her mouth, but Gabe laid a finger across her lips. "No argument. Go."

He grinned as she did what he said. This was going to be fun.

~

Simone's lips tingled from Gabe's touch. She remembered their one kiss and wondered if she'd let him kiss her again. If he wanted to, that is. He set the boundary of their relationship. Friends.

She found a two-top and watched as Gabe leaned over to inspect the glass-enclosed ice cream displays. Did she trust him enough to not get her something outrageous? She'd caught a glimpse of a flavor containing black pepper. Hard no on that one. She could always dump it in the garbage if the flavor he picked was disgusting.

While she waited, Simone considered DavidJon's offer. The salary he offered may not be enough to cover the increased cost of living in Beaverton. A cursory search after DavidJon's first phone call showed the rent for a two-bedroom apartment would cost about fifty percent more of what she currently paid in Main. She'd also have an increase in car insurance and gas.

Time for some serious prayer. *Thanks for the reminder, Granny.*

Gabe walked toward the table with a huge grin. "I got you something you're gonna love," he stated.

"We'll see. What is it?"

"Uh-uh. Taste it first." Gabe handed her one of the waffle cones.

"This must weigh two pounds!" Simone turned the cone around to inspect the two scoops perched precariously on top of each other. She stuck out her tongue and took a tentative swipe across the lilac-colored top scoop. "Not bad."

"Guess what flavor," Gabe said, dropping onto the seat across from her.

Simone closed her eyes. "I'm going to say lavender mixed with something else." She took a bite of the top scoop and moaned. "Oh. My. Goodness. This is so good."

"Chocolate Gooey Brownie on the bottom. Lavender mint on top. I got the same."

Simone's taste buds perked up and sang hallelujah at the explosion of yumminess. "So good," she repeated.

"Told you," Gabe said with a smug smile.

Simone decided against a sarcastic retort. After all, the guy did pay for her ice cream.

"Do you think I'll be in good enough shape for the stair challenge?"

The sudden change of subject took Simone by

surprise. "I think so. It really is up to you. I can help with the physical training, but you have to prepare yourself mentally."

"Not sure what you mean." Gabe's tongue caught a drip down the side of the waffle cone.

Simone thought about her answer. "Have you heard about the Camino de Santiago in Spain?" At Gabe's quick head shake, she continued. "It's this trek in Spain, like a pilgrimage. Remember the movie 'The Way'?" Simone paused to see if Gabe was listening. "Anyway, there are several routes, but the one I was going to do with …" Her voice faltered. "I was going to do the north Camino, which is about four hundred and ninety miles. I figured it would take me about five to six weeks to complete the walk."

Gabe lowered his cone and stared. "Why would you do that?"

Simone shrugged. "Why would you walk up a hundred and ten flights of stairs?"

Gabe nodded. "You have a point."

"Anyway, not only did I have to physically prepare, I had to prepare my mind for the walk. Lots of altitude changes, living out of a backpack, not to mention the language barrier."

"Why didn't you do it?"

Simone decided the best answer would be the direct one. "It was going to be my honeymoon trip. After the wedding that I didn't have."

"Ouch." Gabe paused to crunch down on the waffle cone. "A honeymoon spent walking for six weeks? Are you crazy?"

Simone grimaced. "Yeah. Maybe that's why he took off."

Gabe laughed. "I can think of better ways to spend a honeymoon."

"It's always been a dream of mine, to complete the Camino. Everyone who's done it says it's a spiritual experience."

"I'm thinking this ice cream is a spiritual experience."

Simone felt a smile tease the corners of her mouth. "I agree."

Gabe pushed the last of his cone into his mouth and chewed. "Ready to head home?"

"Sure." Simone carried the rest of her ice cream in one hand and a wad of napkins in the other. By the time they reached Gabe's truck, she'd polished off the last bit of the waffle cone. "That was amazing. Thank you."

Gabe helped her into the truck. "Now that I know your addiction to ice cream, what other secrets might I get you to share?"

Simone's pulse quickened. Her secret at that moment was her growing attraction for this slightly arrogant glory hog. He made her laugh and made her think, and the best part was he made her forget Adam. That was a secret she would have to keep for a while longer. At least until she was confident he felt the same.

Chapter 28

Simone's face held a look Gabe couldn't decipher, like she had a secret. What other secrets was she holding. Gabe wanted to dig deeper into this many-faceted woman. What was her motivation for doing a six-week hike across the top of Spain? She could have a spiritual experience closer to home and a lot less grueling.

He walked around the back of the truck and climbed into the cab. Simone sat with her hands folded in her lap, staring out the windshield.

"What are you thinking?" he asked.

Her sigh was long and drawn-out. "I was thinking about my sister."

Gabe felt a pang of sympathy. "How's she doing?"

"My mom sent me a text last night. They got to Fargo okay. Olivia is having some tests done today. Mom said she'd text me tonight. I think they're an hour later than us."

"You're worried." It wasn't a question.

Simone nodded. "I've been praying. But I can't help worrying."

"You've got a lot on your plate," Gabe commented. "Look, if you don't think you have the bandwidth to finish my training, I can let you off the hook." He hoped she wouldn't take him up on his offer. He let out a small sigh when she told him no.

"It helps me to stay busy," Simone said. "Have you thought much about the offer from the fire department here?"

"Yeah, a lot. I have no idea what to do."

"I hear ya. I feel the same. I'm going home and making a list of pros and cons. That usually helps me sort things out."

"Hm. I never thought of that. If one side outweighs the other, then that's what you do?"

"If only it were that easy. I make the list and consider every option. Usually by the time I finish, I know which way to go, even if the cons outweigh the pros."

"Interesting." Gabe glanced sideways at her. "Where does prayer come into it?"

Simone shot him a surprised look. "You're asking about prayer? I thought . . . Never mind what I thought."

Gabe opted for a teasing tone. "You thought I was a heathen. I will have you know I go to church. Well, I've been to church once since I've been back home. But I pray."

Gabe glanced sideways to see Simone's eyes focused on him, weighing his words.

"I'm serious," he said. "As a matter of fact, God and I are like this." He twisted his index and middle finger together.

Simone shook her head with a tiny smile. "Whatever."

"I'll tell you what. I promise to pray for you to

make the right decision about this job offer if you promise to do the same for me. Deal?" He stuck out his hand.

Simone took it and gave it a shake. "Just be sure you don't make a promise you can't keep, Glory."

Gabe stopped at a traffic light in downtown Salem and leaned across the bench seat. He placed a kiss on Simone's lips. "Sealed with a kiss." He half expected her to shove him away. When she didn't, he kissed her again.

A horn honk behind them snapped his head up. The light had changed to green.

"Oops."

~

Simone's lips tingled when Gabe pulled away. A jumble of thoughts whirled in her head. His kiss incited feelings she'd buried since Adam's departure. Half of her wanted more, but the other half screamed *danger*. She was falling and powerless to stop.

Gabe made her laugh and challenged her the way Adam never had. She'd felt loved and accepted when Adam proposed. The familiar feelings of being not good enough, not pretty enough, returned with a vengeance when he broke their engagement. His family never really accepted her.

Gabe's family was different. His mom seemed to genuinely accept her. The problem was, Gabe's life seemed to be heading in one direction and hers another.

Simone felt her cell vibrate and pulled it from her purse.

"What is it?" Gabe asked.

"It's a text from my mom." Simone said, staring at the screen. "She wants to know if I can stop by the house and check on her plants. The house sitter had some sort of emergency and is going to be gone a couple of days." Simone glanced toward Gabe. "Do you mind if we stop? It's on the way to Main."

"No problem. Give me the directions."

Simone directed him through downtown Salem and down Commercial Street toward South Salem.

Gabe chuckled. "This isn't exactly on the way to Main."

"Okay, so I exaggerated a little," Simone said. "It isn't far. Turn left."

She directed him turn by turn until they pulled up in front of an older home in an established neighborhood. The house had been recently painted an oyster white with green trim. Mature trees spread a welcoming cover, offering shade to the house and home to twittering birds.

"This is it," Simone said.

Gabe turned off the ignition. "Nice house. Is this where you grew up?"

"No. I grew up in Main. My folks moved here after I graduated. My dad got tired of the commute and my mom wanted to be closer to healthcare for my sister."

"Do you have a key?"

Simone held up her key ring and jingled it. They climbed out of the truck and walked up the front walk.

"I'll just be a few minutes," Simone said. "Make sure the plants haven't expired and check that the sprinklers in the yard are working. Help yourself to something to drink."

Gabe gave her a mock salute and wandered into the kitchen.

Simone checked all the plants and gave a few needy

ones a drink of water. She found Gabe standing on the back porch, staring out at the fenced-in yard.

"What are you looking at?" she asked.

Gabe turned, startled by her voice. "The house feels, I don't know, homey."

Simone crossed her arms and leaned on the porch railing. "I know what you mean. I've always felt like every home has a personality. When I was growing up, I visited some of my friends' homes …" She made a face. "I wouldn't want to live there."

"I know exactly what you mean. Your parents' house feels like a home. What did you think of my parents' house?"

Simone smiled, remembering the warmth she'd felt when walking through Debbie's living room. "I loved it. You were lucky to grow up there."

Gabe's eyebrows shot up. "Lucky? Don't you mean blessed?"

"Well, that too."

Gabe reached for her and Simone let him pull her toward him. His hands rested lightly on her upper arms. She stared into his blue eyes, trying to read his expression. Her eyes traveled down his face to his mouth. Would he kiss her again? Would she let him?

~

Gabe's heart raced as he watched a storm of emotions flicker in Simone's eyes. Without hesitation, he lowered his head and captured her lips in a passionate kiss. She melted into him, her body pressing against his. He was playing with fire and was powerless to stop. This was everything he had ever wanted—a connection that grew stronger with every touch, igniting an all-consuming love deep within their souls.

Love? His heart stopped. He was falling in love with Simone. How could that be since he'd only known her for a couple of weeks?

Simone pulled back and raised her eyes to his. "We can't do this." She stepped away and turned to stare into the distance.

Gabe's arms dropped to his sides. "I'm not going to say I'm sorry."

Simone crossed her arms against her stomach. "What are we doing here, Gabe?"

He waved a hand across the expanse of the yard. "We're checking on your parents' plants."

Simone sent him a stink-eye. "That's not what I mean, and you know it."

Gabe turned and leaned back against the porch railing, crossing his feet at the ankles. He rubbed a hand through his hair. "I haven't the slightest idea."

Simone didn't respond. She sank onto a padded wicker chair and put her hands over her face.

She better not be crying.

Gabe leaned toward her. "Are you okay?" Please don't be crying.

Simone dropped her hands and looked up at him. "I'm fine. Let's go." She sprang to her feet and headed into the house.

Gabe hesitated a moment before following her.

They didn't speak until they were seated in Gabe's truck with their seatbelts fastened.

Simone stared out the windshield. "We can't keep doing that. Kissing. We are supposed to be friends. Friends don't do that."

Gosh, she sounded like kissing him was excruciatingly painful. His ego took a direct hit from her words.

"I'm sorry it was so bad for you," Gabe said.

She let out a long sigh. "That's the problem. It wasn't bad."

Chapter 29

Simone's stomach tightened as she turned to face him. "The thing is, you have your life and I have mine. We are heading in opposite directions."

Gabe's grip on the steering wheel tightened until his knuckles turned white. "What if—"

Simone made a sound to stop him.

"No, Simone, hear me out. What if there's something here and we miss it? What if you move to Beaverton and I go back to Portland? We won't be that far apart."

Simone spun her ring around and around, considering her words. The last thing she wanted was to fall in love with someone and have her heart shattered. Again. Gabe had experienced the world and all the fleshly pleasures that came with it. What if it wasn't enough for him? What if *she* wasn't enough? He already admitted to applying for a position all the way across the country. When he tired of her, would he try again?

"What if I decide to stay in Main and you go back to your job? What then?" Simone asked.

"What if I don't go back to my old job?"

Simone let out a groan. "Can we not talk about this

right now? I need to let my mom know we checked on her plants.”

She sent a short text to her mom letting her know all was well at the house. Mom responded with a thumb’s up emoji.

“The wind’s shifted again,” Gabe said, pointing out the driver’s side window. “Look at that smoke.”

The sky in Northern Oregon had been gray with smoke from the fires, but the closer they got to Main, the gray turned to angry red.

Gabe reached for the controls to change the air conditioner from outside air to recirculating.

“Looks like it’s getting closer,” Gabe said.

He slowed the truck as a line of cars snaked in front of them on the highway.

Simone’s eyes burned and her throat felt raw. She squinted through the windshield.

Gabe’s phone blared out a jarring ringtone. He punched the Bluetooth button. Simone saw the name on the screen. ‘Dad.’

“Are you on your way home?” his dad asked.

“We’re on 22, just before the split.”

“Good. I need your help. The fire is burning close to here. Your mom and I are moving the irrigation system closer to the edge of the property. I can see the flames from the edge of our property.”

“Dad, be careful. Where are the twins?”

“Your mom took them to the pastor’s house. Grace is alone at the house. Can you stop by and check on her before you join us?”

Simone watched as Gabe’s face tightened. “I’ll go with you,” she said. “I’ll keep Grace company.”

Gabe nodded. “I’ll be there as soon as I can, Dad.

Traffic is crawling."

Several emergency vehicles, including fire trucks and ambulances, passed them on the shoulder. Gabe's breath came in short audible gasps.

"I need to get home."

Simone began to pray, asking that Gabe's family seed farm would be spared, and that Grace would be okay. She couldn't imagine how awful it would be if Grace went into labor while their house caught fire. Grace must be terrified.

Up ahead, cars were turning around at a roadblock.

"They're not letting anyone into town," Gabe said.

Vehicles ahead of them pulled into the oncoming lane and sped back toward Salem. The gap in front of Gabe's truck widened. He sped forward and reached the blockade.

He rolled his window down to speak to the officer holding his hand up to keep them from going any further.

"Oh, great," Gabe said. "It's your friend Carl the Cop."

Carl the Tool was more like it. Carl approached Gabe's vehicle.

"No one is allowed past this point," Carl said.

Gabe heard the click of Simone's seatbelt as she unlatched it. She scooted over and leaned across Gabe to speak.

"Carl, please let us through. The fire is heading toward Gabe's farm and his sister is alone at the house. She's nine months pregnant. Please."

"I'm sorry, Simone. No can do."

Gabe opened his mouth to speak, but Simone cut him off.

"Carl, look. Gabe is a firefighter. He can help. If Grace goes into labor alone, it's on you. Let us through. Now."

Carl sent Gabe a hard look, then relented. "Fine." Carl moved the sawhorse blockade barely wide enough for Gabe's pickup. Gabe crept through the narrow opening, then jammed on the accelerator.

"Thanks," he said.

Simone stayed in the middle of the bench seat with her thigh pressed against his. Her warmth soothed him despite the tension filling his chest.

"Carl is a good guy. A little rough around the edges. But he's okay."

Gabe shot her a look. "So, do you plan to go out with him again?"

Simone grimaced. "Uh, no. He's a bit clingy."

Sweet relief. He should have known Simone wasn't the type to kiss one guy and go out with another.

His truck tires spun as he took the turn onto his parents' drive. The truck bounced over the uneven gravel. He skidded to a stop in front of the house.

"Text me and let me know how Grace is, okay?"

Simone nodded and leaned over to reach for the door handle. "And you let me know about the fire, okay?"

Gabe gave a terse nod. Simone paused in the doorway and turned to give him a small wave. He raised his hand and turned the wheel toward the fields.

~

Simone let herself into the silent house. "Hello? Grace?"

She tiptoed down the hall off the living room, hoping to find Grace sleeping. The air inside smelled of smoke and lavender. An oil diffuser sat on the coffee table, spewing out the fragrance. It did little to mask the scent of the fires pressing against the windows.

The whole landscape held an eerie semi-darkness. The trees shading the backyard were barely visible through the kitchen windows.

The first bedroom on the right was obviously Gabe's. Clothes were strewn on the bed and a half-drunk bottle of water sat on the nightstand. She found Grace lying on the bed in the bedroom across the hall from Gabe's.

Her eyes slid open when Simone entered the room.

"Simone?" Grace said. Her voice was slurred.

Simone approached the bed and stared down at Grace's flushed face.

"Thirsty," Grace mumbled.

"I'll get some water."

Simone hustled into the kitchen and found a clean glass in the cupboard over the dishwasher. She filled the glass with ice and water from the dispenser on the fridge.

"Here, drink some of this," Simone said, returning to the bedroom.

Grace struggled to sit up enough to take the glass. She guzzled half the water before lying back.

"I'm hot."

Simone walked to the wall switches, pushing one and then another until she found the control for the overhead fan. She turned it on high and returned to the bed. "What else can I get you?"

Grace eyes radiated pain "I'm having contractions."

Her words filled Simone with terror. "I'll call 9-1-1."

The emergency operator told Simone it would be difficult to get an ambulance to the house, due to the wildfire.

"But I can walk you through the birth process," the operator offered.

"Let's hope it doesn't come to that," Simone murmured. A sudden beeping burst through Simone's cell phone as the call disconnected.

Panic gripped her as she tried to redial 9-1-1. Busy. She tried again. Busy.

Grace gabbed for Simone's hand and squeezed. "Don't leave me."

"I won't." She couldn't leave anyway. She had no vehicle. "What can I do?"

Grace groaned and pressed on her bulging tummy. She panted until the contraction passed. "Talk to me. Where are my girls?"

Simone clenched and unclenched her hand when Grace released it. Her grip was vice-like.

"Gabe said they're at your pastor's house."

Grace nodded. "Okay. Did you spend the day with my brother?" Another gasp. "Feel this," Grace said, taking Simone's hand and placing it on her stomach."

Simone felt the muscles in Grace's abdomen tighten. "Wow. How bad does it hurt?"

Grace exhaled when the contraction passed. "Not too bad. A little like menstrual cramps. Not like the twins. That was brutal." She shifted on the bed to get more comfortable. "Keep talking. Tell me what you and Gabe did today."

Simone thought back to earlier that day. Was it only a few hours ago that she and Gabe headed to Beaverton?

"Gabe drove me to Beaverton for a job interview." Simone talked about her long friendship with DavidJon, the boutique gym he was opening, and his offer.

When another contraction passed, Grace asked, "Are you going to take the job?"

"I don't know."

Grace closed her eyes and settled back against the pile of pillows behind her. Simone thought she'd fallen asleep.

"Do you like my brother?" Grace's eyes remained closed.

"Yes."

Grace's voice softened to a whisper. "Maybe you should take the job. You'll be sort of close to where Gabe lives."

That was part of the problem. Grace must not know about Gabe's offer from the Main Fire Department.

Simone kept her eyes on Grace's face, which gradually relaxed. Perhaps her labor had stopped. Simone slid to her feet and stepped to a comfy-looking chair near the door.

Her phone showed no service except for SOS. What a joke. She couldn't even reach 9-1-1. No chance there'd be a text from Gabe either.

The late afternoon sky resembled something from a dystopian movie. It was dark enough to be nine at night and the smoky haze covered everything like fog. Simone's nose tickled from the bits of ash filtering through every crevice of Gabe's house. The air was deadly silent. No birds chirped outside. She and Grace were cocooned in a dusky haze.

Simone was reminded of the story of Shadrach, Meshach, and Abednego in the fiery furnace. Those three Hebrew boys survived the flames and came out without even smelling of smoke. Would she and Grace survive their own fiery furnace?

She ran through several scenarios. One, Gabe and his parents returned and took Grace to the hospital. Two, the house caught fire and she and Grace died. Simone shuddered. Why did she always go to the worst-case scenario?

You're going to be fine.

A sudden cry from Grace snapped her out of her thoughts. She was not going to be fine. Grace was going to give birth and Simone had no idea what to do.

Chapter 30

Gabe reached the edge of his parents' property and shoved the truck into Park. Heat from the nearby fire pushed against the bare skin of his arms and legs. Cursing himself for not grabbing his gear from the house, he ran to where his mom struggled with the arms of the massive sprinkler.

"Let me help." Mom turned to him with a look of relief. Sweat ran down the sides of her face, wetting her tee shirt. Her hair was matted with gray flecks of ash.

"Where's dad?"

Mom pointed in the distance. Gabe could barely make out his dad's form through the thick haze.

Together he and his mom rotated the equipment to face outward rather than toward their property. She worked on one end and he on the other to rotate the spray.

"Step back," Gabe shouted. He found the switch and waited for the water to begin spurting out through the spigots.

Usually, the force of the spray would be enough to cause burns or bruising. But with the amount of pressure they used today, the spray only launched a few feet. Gabe hoped it would be enough.

Gabe strode to where his mom stood watching the water douse the dry ground. She grabbed him in a fierce hug before letting him go.

"Let's go to Dad," Gabe said.

"I'm so glad you're here," Mom said, taking Gabe's hand. "How is Grace?"

"I don't know. I dropped Simone off at the house. She's supposed to text me." He pulled his cell phone from his back pocket. No service.

"I'm worried about her," Mom said. "She wasn't feeling well this morning. I should have sent her with the girls to Pastor Roy's house."

"Don't worry, Mom. Simone will take good care of her."

"But what if she goes into labor?" Mom sent him a worried look.

"It'll be fine." But would it? Sure, Simone could do CPR, as evidenced by the motorcycle accident. But did she have basic medical training like he did? What if Grace had the baby and Simone was not able to help?

He shot a glance heavenward into the musty sky. God, please take care of Grace and Simone.

They found Gabe's dad at the edge of their land, a shovel in one hand and the other holding his baseball cap. He turned when they approached.

"I think we're going to be okay," he said. He coughed and spit. "Gah. This ash is killing me."

The three stood and watched the smoke rising in the distance as live embers floated toward them in the breeze.

In the distance, Gabe could barely make out the shape of firetrucks with their hoses pointed directly into the fire. He knew from experience that sometimes the flames were so hot the water evaporated as soon as it left the hose. His heart quickened with envy for those guys on the front line. Why was he here when he should be helping his fellow responders?

He should be out there, not here. At that moment his life seemed trivial. All the training for the stair challenge when he could have been back at his home station preparing for real life.

His mom's words echoed in his head. "I'm glad you're here."

If he wasn't here, he wouldn't have been able to help on the farm. Back in Portland, he wouldn't have met Simone. What was happening back at the house? He wiped sweat from his forehead with the back of one hand. Grace had to be okay. Simone too.

"Watch out!" Dad's shout snapped Gabe back to the present. A gust of wind deposited a bunch of burning embers onto the dry grass beyond the dirt fire break. The brush burst into flames.

~

Simone wandered into the kitchen to peer out into the smoky haze. The air conditioner kicked on, its low hum the only sound in the silent house. She sent up a prayer for protection for Gabe and his parents. If only she knew what was happening out there. Were they safe? Was the fire coming closer to the house?

She checked her phone again, hoping for a word from Gabe or her mom. What news was there about Olivia? Simone was cut off from the rest of the world with no way to know where the fire was headed or how her sister was doing.

Wiping sweaty palms down her shorts, she wandered into the living room. The darkness of the sky cast a depressing shadow over the room. She turned on a lamp and took in the spacious room and was hit with a wave of homesickness for her folks' house. The two houses weren't similar, but they felt the same. Warm, cozy, and inviting. What were Mom and Dad doing right now? How was Olivia holding up? If only she could talk to Mom. She'd know what to do.

A loud cry from the bedroom stirred Simone into action. She raced into Grace's room. Grace's eyes squeezed closed as she panted through another contraction.

When it passed, she took a breath and let it out. "The contractions stopped for a few minutes. I must have dozed off. They're back with a vengeance."

"What can I do?" Simone's voice rose an octave.

"Help me out of these clothes." She'd raised her tee shirt halfway. "Grab a nightgown from the second drawer.

Simone did as she was told and handed Grace the nightgown, turning to give her some privacy.

"Help me with my shorts," Grace said, dropping her shirt and bra on the floor.

Grace lay back while Simone pulled the maternity shorts over Grace's taut belly. Grace lifted her hips so Simone could slide them off. She pulled the nightgown down.

"How about a sip of water?" Simone asked when Grace was settled again.

"Sure. Then grab some rag towels from the linen closet in the hall." Grace was all business now. "Spread the towels over the bed, under me. Grab my mom's scissors from her sewing cabinet in the room at the end of the hall. You'll need to sterilize them. And grab two clothespins from the laundry room."

Simone's hands shook as she found the scissors where Grace said. Carrying them into the kitchen with sweaty fingers, she laid them on the counter and searched through cupboards until she found a pot. Filling it with water, she set it on the stove to boil while searching the laundry room for the requested clothespins. She was hit with a swoop of vertigo as the enormity of the situation hit her like a tsunami.

"Breathe," she said aloud. "You can do this."

When she returned to Grace's room, she found her writhing through another contraction. Simone used a towel to dry Grace's wet forehead.

"Did your water break?" Simone asked.

Grace shook her head. "No, but that doesn't surprise me. It didn't with the twins either. They were so low that all the fluid was behind them. I think this guy is the same."

"The water's heating," Simone said, more to keep Grace talking than for information.

Grace reached for Simone's hand. "We can do this. Women have been giving birth since the garden of Eden."

Simone wished she had the same level of confidence as Gabe's sister. What if the baby came and he didn't start breathing? What if he got stuck in the birth canal? What if . . . A dozen possibilities jammed her consciousness. What if she was responsible for the baby dying? Or Grace bleeding to death?

"Stop worrying," Grace said, tightening her grip on Simone's already bruised fingers. "I know it's going to be okay."

I hope so.

Chapter 31

Gabe's dad used his shovel to pour dirt over live embers dancing in the breeze and landing near his feet.

"Go back to the house and fill some buckets with water."

Gabe hesitated only a second before racing back to his pickup. He skidded to a stop behind the house, not caring that he'd driven over Mom's prized lawn. He found two five-gallon paint buckets in the shed and set them to fill.

Sticking his head through the kitchen door, he listened for any sound coming from the house. Hearing none, he grabbed the buckets and returned to his truck. The girls must be napping. Good.

He drove back more slowly to keep the water from sloshing out of the buckets and onto the floor of his truck.

Hard to believe only an hour or so ago, he and Simone sat side by side in this very cab, talking about their future.

~

Grace's panting became interspersed with groans and cries of pain. Simone stood by, wringing her hands. She pulled the chair closer to the bed, leaning forward to wipe the sweat off Grace's forehead.

"What else can I do?"

Grace cracked open her eyes. "Just be here." She swallowed back a sob. "I don't know what I'd do if I were alone."

"Want me to time the contractions?" Simone offered.

"Sure. Whatever. It doesn't matter. This little guy is coming soon."

Simone wracked her brain for something to say. "Have you and your husband decided on a name?"

Grace blew short breaths through pursed lips. "Demarcus wants to name him Derek."

"And you?"

"I'm fine with it. But I picked his middle name. John."

"Derek John. I like it."

Simone jumped when Grace screeched. "Oh, my goodness!" She let out a wail and grabbed her stomach with both hands.

Simone jumped up, adrenaline pulsing. She ran to the kitchen and dropped the scissors into the boiling water. How long did it take to sanitize scissors? She'd completely forgotten the science she'd learned in college.

She leaned over the sink, fighting a wave of nausea.

Don't lose it now.

The woman in the other room needed her. Depended on her. Suck it up, buttercup. Put on your big girl panties and help Grace give birth to Derek John.

~

Gabe and his parents raced from ember to ember, dousing the spurts of flames with water or dirt. The wind finally died and with it the floating sparks. Gabe rested both hands on his thighs and coughed. He and his parents took turns sharing the remaining water in the buckets to soothe their burning throats.

Gabe's mom wiped tears from her face, leaving black streaks of ash like macabre face painting.

"I'm so relieved," she said between sobs. "I hope our neighbors are okay."

Gabe pulled his phone out again. "We won't know until we get back to the house. I've got no service."

"We'll use the satellite radio," Dad said. He draped an arm across Gabe's aching shoulders. "Good work, Son."

Gabe's heart swelled under his dad's approval. He'd missed that feeling since his relationship with Tiffany. But he was back in his parents' graces, and back under God's grace. It felt good.

Now, what to do about his future?

Mom pulled off her gloves and dropped them on the ground. "Let's go back to the house and check on Grace."

She followed Gabe's dad to where they'd parked their beat-up old flatbed. Gabe's steps were leaden as he walked back to his truck. He climbed in and leaned his head against the steering wheel. He was weary to the bone, both physically and emotionally. The adrenaline surge from keeping the fire away from the property had dissipated, leaving him exhausted.

It was a familiar feeling. One he craved.

Gabe and his parents arrived at the house at the same time. His dad stumbled from the cab of the truck, then righted himself. When had his parents gotten old? They needed family around. They needed him around, to help and to watch out for them.

Once Grace's husband Demarcus returned from overseas, they'd move on to his next assignment. Mom and Dad would be left alone. Again.

Guilt twisted a knife in Gabe's gut. He'd been so wrapped up in his own life he'd neglected his family. With a burst of clarity, he decided to accept Derek's job offer and stay in Main. Near his parents.

The only problem was, what if Simone decided to move to Beaverton?

Gabe's mom stepped ahead of the men and got to the back door first. By the time Gabe and his dad entered the kitchen, his mom was already down the hall toward the bedrooms.

Gabe moved to the sink to wash his hands and face. His head was partially underwater when he heard his mom's squeal.

"John! Gabe! Come here!"

Gabe grabbed a towel and rubbed it across his head as he hurried to Grace's room. What he saw stopped him cold.

"Meet your new grandson." Simone held a tiny bundle toward Gabe's mom.

In the distance, Gabe heard the wail of an ambulance.

"Is she . . ." He took in his sister's flushed face and closed eyes.

"I'm fine," Grace said, cracking open her eyes.

Simone smiled. "I was finally able to get a signal. The ambulance is taking her to the hospital as a precaution." She leaned toward him and said in a whisper, "I've never delivered a baby before."

Simone's face glowed with pride.

Mom reached for the baby then jerked back. "I have to go wash my hands."

"Me too," Dad echoed.

Gabe glanced from Simone to his sister and back to Simone. "Wow."

"Wow is right," Simone said, nestling the baby against her cheek.

Gabe suddenly felt too gritty to be in the same room with a newborn. "I'm gonna get cleaned up. Then I'll be back to hold my nephew." He took a step back. "It is a boy, right?"

Grace waved a languid hand. "Derek John." Her eyes closed again even as she held out her arms for the infant.

Simone laid the baby on Grace's chest and followed Gabe out of the bedroom. In the hall, Simone grabbed his arm. He could practically smell the adrenaline oozing from her pores.

"Oh my goodness, that was so amazing. A miracle, really. I can't believe we did it. Well, Grace did most of the work, but still—"

"I'd hug you if I weren't covered in ash," Gabe said, smiling down at her.

"I'm so amped up I can hardly stand it. Maybe I should try a second career as a birth doula."

"Birth doula?" What was she talking about?

"Yes! That would be so cool. I could coach mothers giving birth through the process. Like a midwife in the olden days."

"Slow down, Simone. Wait for the adrenaline high to fade before you make any rash decisions."

She furrowed her brow. "It's not like I'm going to run out and enroll in doula school this instant. If there is such a thing, anyway. But, seriously, what an amazing experience of God's life-giving miracle. Your sister did so awesome."

Gabe chuckled at Simone's enthusiasm. "You hold that thought right there while I jump in the shower." He leaned toward her and planted a quick kiss on her lips. "There. Hardly any soot got on you."

Simone squealed and wiped her hand across her lips. "I'm going to kill you."

Gabe dashed into his bedroom and closed the door before she could get near enough to do bodily harm.

Twenty minutes later, he stepped out of the bathroom with his hair still damp. It took three applications of shampoo before all the soot was out of his hair. Gabe craved that feeling of clean after responding to a fire and sweating like a pig inside his gear.

He found Simone lying on the living room sofa with her head on one of the armrests.

"Where is everybody?"

Simone stirred and sat up, rubbing her eyes. "Your parents followed the ambulance to the hospital. I told them I'd wait here for you. I actually can't go anywhere because my car is still at my apartment." She opened her mouth in a huge yawn. "Gosh I'm tired."

"C'mon, I'll take you home."

~

Who knew helping someone give birth could be so exhausting? Simone's steps dragged as she followed Gabe out to his truck. She paused with one foot on the running board.

She jumped when Gabe's voice sounded in her ear. "Need some help?"

"Please."

Gabe took hold of her left arm and hefted her into his pickup.

"Thanks." She leaned her head back against the seat and closed her eyes. She opened them only when Gabe reached across her to fasten her seatbelt.

Her eyes flew open when Gabe said, "Did you know you snore when you're asleep?"

Simone couldn't believe they were already at her apartment. She must have dozed off. "Do not," she retorted.

"Uh, yeah you do."

Simone's foggy brain couldn't come up with a response. Her bed was calling her name. Loudly and insistently.

"Thanks for the ride." Simone barely spared Gabe a glance as she slid from the truck and stumbled to her front door. The key refused to go into the lock, despite her attempts to stab it in.

"Let me help," Gabe said, pulling the keys from her grasp.

Simone leaned against him as he helped her into the apartment. "So tired," she mumbled.

Gabe wrapped one arm around her shoulders and used the other one to close the door behind him.

"Bedroom?" he asked.

Simone raised a shaking hand and pointed down the hall. He supported her weight until they reached her bedroom.

"So tired," Simone said as Gabe deposited her on the bed.

"It's the aftermath of the adrenaline. You'll be fine after a nice nap."

Simone closed her eyes and sank onto the pillow. She felt rather than saw Gabe pull a soft throw over her. "Thanks, glory. You're all right."

Chapter 32

Gabe stared down at Simone's sleeping form. She'd be out for at least an hour, maybe more. He stumbled back to her living room. The same weariness she was experiencing hit him. The long drive to Portland and back. Protecting his parents' property. Learning that he was an uncle again.

He sent a text to his mom.

I'll be home later. Keep me posted on Grace.

Her thumbs up response was enough. Gabe sank onto Simone's couch and pulled over a decorative pillow. A few minutes of shut-eye before he drove home was in order. He was asleep in seconds.

He woke to the sound of ice clinking in a glass. He shot up and looked around the room. Where was he?

Simone appeared in the door leading to the kitchen. "Hey, Glory, did you know you snore?" Her grin challenged him to deny it.

"Do not."

"Do too." Simone waved her phone at him. "Want to hear the recording?"

Gabe jumped up and lunged for her phone, but

Simone was quick. She clenched the phone to her stomach and bent over. Gabe pulled her against his chest and tickled her until she begged him to stop.

Gasping for breath and laughing, Simone said. "I didn't record it, you brute."

Gabe pulled his shirt down and smoothed it over his chest. "See that you don't."

Her grin was sly. "But if I did …"

He shot out a hand to tickle her again but she laughed and retreated into the kitchen.

"I was working on some food. I don't know about you, but I'm starving."

Gabe thought back to the last time he'd eaten. It must have been the ice cream at Salt and Straw. "What are you making?"

"Grilled cheese sandwiches and tomato soup. Comfort food for poor people."

"Sounds good to me. Make me two."

Simone waved the butter knife at him. "What's the magic word?"

Gabe grasped his hands together. "Please."

"Okay, but I'm going to have a talk with your mom about your manners."

This. This is what he missed in his relationship with Tiffany. Theirs had been based on passion. Not friendship. No friendly bantering and definitely no silly tickling. This reminded him of his parents. Watching them throughout his teen years had taught him how married people behaved. Why he'd thrown it away to pursue Tiffany was still a mystery.

A Scripture verse came to mind. "The heart is deceitful above all things and desperately wicked. Who can know it?" (Jeremiah 17:9 NKJV)

He watched Simone lay three sandwiches in a fry pan and search in a cupboard for a carton of organic tomato soup. Her movements were smooth and efficient. There was nothing artificial about Simone. Outwardly, she portrayed 'what you see is what you get.' But Gabe wanted to dig deeper. What were her fears, her losses? What made her sad, happy, emotional?

Being with Simone wasn't about her being hot. It wasn't about lusting after her and desiring to take her physically. There were sparks between them, but Gabe knew sparks die and can turn to ash.

Simone was beautiful. Driven. Talented. And Gabe loved her.

A gust of emotion caught him by surprise. He was in love with her.

He'd feared Simone was another Tiffany. It was a cliché, but Simone made him want to be a better person. A better Christian. A man worthy of her affection. Her love.

~

Simone felt Gabe's gaze burning into her back as she stood over the sizzling pan, preparing their dinner. She tried to ignore it, but deep down, she couldn't deny the flutter of excitement it caused. Ever since they had met, there had been an undeniable chemistry between them, and Simone found herself constantly yearning for more.

But then there was Adam, the man who had broken off their engagement without warning and left her heart shattered. His sudden departure had brought back painful memories of past judgments and discrimination she faced because of her mixed-race background.

Despite her outward confidence, Simone still carried the scars of those experiences, always wondering if people were secretly judging her or making snide remarks behind her back. And now with Gabe's lingering presence in her apartment, those doubts resurfaced once again, leaving her torn between moving on and holding onto the hurt from the past.

Simone's hands trembled slightly as she flipped the sizzling sandwiches, her mind a whirlwind of conflicting emotions. She glanced over at Gabe, leaning against the kitchen counter, watching her with an intensity that made her heart race.

As the aroma of melting cheese filled the room, Simone couldn't help but feel a sense of unease creeping over her. She knew that Gabe was different from Adam. Kinder, more empathetic, and attentive in a way that made her feel seen and understood. But could she really let go of the pain and betrayal Adam had caused her?

Lost in her thoughts, Simone nearly jumped when Gabe spoke up, his voice gentle yet firm. "Simone, I—" His phone rang. With a groan, he retrieved it from where it lay on the kitchen table. "It's my mom."

Simone sent him a 'go ahead and take it' wave.

"I'll put it on speaker," Gabe said. "Mom, how is Grace?"

"Exhausted. Happy. Can you believe they're sending her home tonight?"

"That's awesome," Gabe said.

"They gave her a few stitches, weighed and measured little Derek and pronounced them fit."

"I'm glad to hear that. And so is Simone." Gabe nodded to her. "I'm here at her place."

"Simone, I can't thank you enough for being at the house and for … everything. Grace said you were amazing."

Simone felt her face grow hot. "Thank you, Debbie."

"You're a hero, my dear."

Simone shrugged, even though she knew Gabe's mom couldn't see her.

Gabe's eyes held hers. "You're right, Mom. Simone is a hero."

Mom's sob sounded through the phone. "I better go before I blubber all over myself. I'm exhausted."

"Get some rest, Mom," Gabe said. "I'll be home a little later."

Simone turned toward the stove and flipped the sandwiches one more time to be sure each side was the correct degree of toastiness. Satisfied, she slid them onto two plates and cut them in half.

"Here, put these on the table and grab a couple of paper towels," Simone said. She poured the soup into two bowls and carried them to the table.

"Let's eat," she said, dropping onto a chair.

Gabe took the chair opposite. "Thanks for this," he said, waving a hand over their food. "Let's say grace. Is that okay with you?"

Simone nodded and bowed her head while Gabe said a short prayer of thanks for their food and for Grace's healthy baby boy. "And thanks for sparing our farm," Gabe added when he was done.

"Amen," Simone echoed. "Tell me about that. How bad was the fire? How close did it come?"

Gabe took a huge bite of his first sandwich and spoke around the food. "The fire wasn't too close, but the wind sent a lot of live embers our way. We spent a lot of energy dousing sparks and floating embers."

Simone shuddered. "Sounds terrifying."

Gabe shrugged. "All in a day's work for me. Not as terrifying as helping my sister give birth."

Simone watched Gabe eat, marveling at how comfortable she was around him. He caught her eye and winked.

"You were pretty hyped up after that. Were you serious about the doula thing?"

Simone set the crust of her sandwich on her plate and wiped her hands. Leaning forward, she said, "Watching little Derek being born made me think. A lot. I've been stuck in this rut for a long time. I wanted to do that Camino de Santiago. I was thinking of it as a distraction, something to look forward to. But that's all it was. A distraction."

"Go on," Gabe said when she stopped.

"In between Grace's contractions, I started thinking about the job offer from DavidJon. I made a list of pros and cons when I got home."

"Yeah?"

Simone pushed back her chair and walked into the living room, returning with a sheet of lined yellow paper. She slid it across the table toward him.

Her hands grew clammy as she watched his eyes move back and forth across the two columned list.

When he reached the bottom, his head jerked up and his eyes pinned hers.

"What's this?" He asked, jabbing a finger on the paper.

Chapter 33

Gabe couldn't believe his eyes. He read through Simone's list of pros and cons twice before tapping his finger on the last item.

Pros:
A change of scenery
New people
More money
Gabe

Cons:
Higher cost of living
Having to make new friends
Gabe

"Why is my name here?" Gabe kept his eyes pinned on hers, hoping for the answer he desperately wanted.

A dozen emotions ran across Simone's face. She dropped her gaze to her lap.

"Stop spinning your promise ring and talk to me. Why am I a 'con.' And a 'pro?'"

Simone swallowed and opened her mouth, closed it, and opened it again. "If I move to Beaverton and you stay here, we won't see each other." Simone glanced around the room before her eyes met his again.

"The thing is … I don't want to be that far away. But I also don't want to keep doing what I'm doing."

Gabe's pulse jumped. "Are you saying you want to stay here and see where this," he waved a finger between the two of them. "Goes?"

Simone nodded. "If you go back to Portland and I move to Beaverton, then we can, you know, see what happens. But if you take the job with Main Fire Department and I stay here, same thing."

"But you're bored."

"I think I want to go back to school."

Now that she said the words out loud, the idea sounded ridiculous. She was twenty-seven years old for goodness' sake. How could she possibly afford it?

"What do you think you want to study?" Gabe's voice held no sarcasm or skepticism.

Simone stared down at her untouched bowl of soup. "I love working with older adults. Something in geriatrics maybe?"

She hazarded a glance at Gabe's face. He nodded. "It's definitely a growing field. You wouldn't believe the number of calls we get to help an older person get up after a fall."

Simone leaned forward. "That's right. I want to help seniors stay fit so they don't keep falling in their own homes. My granny still lives by herself in Georgia and she's almost ninety."

Gabe's eyebrows rose. "That's awesome."

Simone sat back with a sigh. "Who am I kidding? I'm too old to go back to school. Besides, how would I afford it?"

Gabe reached across the table and grabbed her

hand. "Hey, stop talking like that. You of all people should know God can make a way."

Simone tightened her lips. *Maybe.*

Gabe finished his soup and stood to carry his bowl and plate to the sink. "I better get home. I'm wasted. Long day. Thanks for dinner."

Simone watched him attempt to smother a yawn. "Next time I'll make something a little more fancy." She stood and reached for her bowl. Before she could pick it up, Gabe's arms were around her.

"I like poor man's comfort food," he said, pulling her head to his chest.

His voice rumbled under her ear. She wanted to keep him talking. "What's your favorite food?"

His chest rose and fell as he breathed. "Steak." Even his one-word answer sent a frisson of comfort through her.

She shivered when he pulled away. He lay a soft kiss on her lips. "See you tomorrow."

He walked into the living room and out the front door. Simone folded her arms across her stomach. Before she could process their conversation, her phone rang.

"Hi, Mom. Is everything okay?"

"Honey, sorry to be calling so late. You are up, aren't you?"

Simone carried the phone into the living room and sank onto the sofa. She pulled the pillow Gabe had been using onto her lap. It still smelled like him. Fresh, slightly smoky, and decidedly male.

"I'm up. How is Olivia?" Simone braced herself for bad news.

"That's why I'm calling. It looks like we're going to

be up here for awhile. Maybe even six months. Dad is going to fly down and pack more clothes and drive the car up here."

"And Olivia?"

"We have a great team of doctors, thank the Lord. They're confident they can take care of the tumor without operating." Mom exhaled into the phone. "I couldn't stand the thought of them drilling into my baby's head. Anyway, Olivia will start the treatments next week."

Simone slumped back against the sofa. "That's great news."

"The thing is," Mom continued. "I don't know what to do about leaving the house empty for that long. It would be a huge imposition for us to ask you to keep an eye on it."

An idea that began as a seed while Gabe slept germinated into a full-blown plan. She could let her apartment go and move into her folks' house. She'd still be close to Main.

And Gabe.

"Mom, I'm thinking of going back to school."

"Really? That's great. What brought that on?"

"Let me tell you about my day."

~

Gabe woke the next morning to the sun streaming past the edges of the blinds. Blinking against the rays, he pulled himself to a sitting position. No sounds came from beyond his closed bedroom door. He must have slept through Grace's return from the hospital.

He pulled on some athletic shorts and padded into the kitchen. Someone, probably Dad, had prepped the coffee maker. He punched the button to start the brew and stared out the kitchen window.

A light rain had fallen during the night, leaving sparkling droplets on the backyard grass. Only a few wisps of gray clouds were left of the haze that had pushed its way West. Gabe breathed a sigh of relief and a prayer of thanks for God's protection on their home.

"God, I want to tell Simone how I feel," he said aloud. His voice echoed in the empty kitchen.

He jumped when his sister's voice spoke behind him.

"Who are you talking to?"

He whirled around, ready to tear into her for scaring him. He clamped down on the words at the sight of his sister, carrying her newborn.

"Can I see him?" Gabe asked. At her nod, he tiptoed across the room to gaze down at the sleeping baby.

"Want to hold him?"

"I'm terrified I'll break him. Or drop him."

Grace laughed. "I dropped you when you were a baby and look how you turned out."

"Did not," Gabe protested. He allowed Grace to transfer the burrito-wrapped Derek into his arms. Gabe couldn't take his eyes off the infant. His skin was light brown and his black hair stood up like a mohawk.

Butterflies danced in Gabe's stomach as he cradled baby Derek, feeling a rush of protectiveness and love he never knew existed. Derek shifted in his arms, wrapping one tiny hand around Gabe's finger, and Gabe could swear he felt his heart grow three sizes in that moment. Grace watched them both with a tender smile, her eyes shining with unshed tears.

"You're a natural, Gabe," she whispered. "Someday, when you have your own baby, you'll be an amazing father."

Gabe looked up at her, the weight of her words settling deep within him. A future he had never dared to imagine now seemed within reach, as he gazed down at the innocent life in his arms. The idea of holding his own child someday filled him with a mixture of excitement and nervousness, but most of all, it filled him with hope. And with thoughts of Simone.

Gabe could barely speak around the tears in his throat. "Thanks, Sis. I take back almost every bad thing I ever said about you."

"Almost every?" Grace said with a smile.

Gabe handed Derek back to his sister. His arms felt unusually empty once the baby was safely transferred.

"Your girlfriend did an amazing job yesterday. I don't know what I would have done if I was here alone. I thought for sure she was going to lose it when we had to cut the umbilical cord." Grace raised one shoulder. "She's a keeper, Gabe."

Gabe was about to protest that Simone wasn't his girlfriend, but he bit back the words. He wanted it to be true. He felt the familiar nudge of the Holy Spirit. The same nudge he'd ignored when he pursued Tiffany, warning him of impending disaster. He'd ignored the nudge then, but he wouldn't now.

"Yes, she's amazing," Gabe agreed. "A real hero."

Chapter 34

Was nine o'clock too early to call Gabe? Maybe if she sent a text first. She'd been up since six, despite the excitement and stress of the previous twenty-four hours. It wasn't every day you helped someone have a baby.

Composing a short text, her finger hovered over the 'send' arrow. Why was Gabe the first person she wanted to tell about her new plan? Anticipation bubbled up into a giggle as she thought about the life changes she was about to make.

Casting aside doubt, Simone pressed Send and waited for the 'Delivered' message to appear. Ten seconds later her phone rang.

"Hope it isn't too early," Simone said.

Gabe chuckled. "Not at all. What's up?"

"I have something I want to tell you." Simone held her breath.

"Good because I have something I want to tell you too. Want to meet me at Human Bean? My treat."

Simone exhaled. "Yes. Give me fifteen minutes."

She should have asked for more time. It took almost ten minutes to tame her curls into submission. It left her only enough time to swipe some berry-colored gloss across her lips before dashing out the door.

She found Gabe seated with two large cups of coffee in front of him. He made a point of looking at this watch as she walked to the table.

"Sorry I'm late," she said in a rush.

He grinned. "No worries." He pushed one of the coffees in her direction.

"Thanks." Simone took a tentative sip. Sugar, no cream. She sent him a questioning glance.

"I'm a trained observer," Gabe said.

A part of Simone she'd thought was dead slowly came to life. Gabe knew her. He remembered how she liked her coffee. He cared.

Telling him she would be moving to Salem to stay in her folks' house would be more difficult than she thought.

Gabe leaned back in his chair. "What did you want to talk about?"

Simone swallowed. "You first."

"Uh uh. You texted me first."

"You called," Simone said.

Gabe shook his head and glanced around the cafe. He sucked in a breath and blew it out. "Two things. One, the City Council is having a ceremony tomorrow evening. They are honoring local heroes. One of them being me."

"Figures," Simone mumbled.

Gabe narrowed his eyes. "Do you read your emails?"

Simone frowned. What did this have to do with her? She spread her arms wide. "I've been a little distracted lately. You know, helping a woman have a baby. Training some glory hog for some stair thing."

"If you'd read your emails, you'd see the City Council wants to honor you too."

"Why?"

Gabe rolled his eyes. "Apparently someone at the hospital told someone else who told the mayor that you were solely responsible for the birth of little Derek John."

~

Gabe watched Simone's eyes widen with disbelief.

"Me?" she asked.

Gabe held his cup in one hand and tipped it toward her. "Now who's a glory hog?"

Simone bit her lip, then smiled. "Cool." She took a drink of coffee and set it down. "What was the second thing?"

"Huh?"

"You said you had two things to tell me."

"It's your turn," Gabe said. He needed to figure out a way to build up to his declaration.

Simone's hands dropped to her lap. He'd bet she was fiddling with her promise ring. Was she about to tell him she'd decided to take her friend up on his job offer? His heart thudded against his ribcage. That would change how he approached things.

Spit it out, Simone. Take me out of my misery.

"I'm moving," she said.

Gabe felt the floor cave under him. She was moving to Beaverton, and he'd be staying here in Main.

"You're taking the job with your friend's gym? That's great." His words sounded hollow, even to himself.

Simone shook her head. "No. Not to Beaverton." She looked at him like he had two heads. "I'm moving into my folks' house in Salem."

Gabe's brain was a jumbled mess. "Why?"

Simone inhaled and said, "I'm going back to school."

Gabe tried to grasp this new information and failed. "Back up. What?"

"Remember I talked about wanting to do something different? I mentioned school."

"Yeah, I thought that was the adrenaline talking. Are you talking about doula school?"

Simone laughed. "No. That was the adrenaline talking. Don't you remember our conversation yesterday about me wanting to work with senior adults?"

Gabe scratched his head and frowned. "I must have been zoned out. I'm sorry."

"Are you paying attention this time?" Simone smiled, taking the sting from her words.

"You have all my attention, ma'am." He leaned forward and rested his elbows on the table.

"I had a long chat with my mom last night. They're going to be in Fargo for at least six months."

Gabe shook his head. "I'm so confused right now."

Simone laughed. "Try to keep up, Glory." She ticked off her fingers one by one. "My folks' house will be empty for six months. They need someone to house sit. I'm going to enroll in OSU and hopefully get enough credits to be accepted into the nursing program. I can save money by staying in their house."

Gabe finally understood. "You're not moving north? You're staying here?"

"As I said, Glory, try to keep up."

They grinned at each other across the table.

~

Gabe's pulse sped up and the pressure in his chest made it difficult to breathe. Simone wasn't leaving.

"What else did you want to tell me?" she asked.

Gabe's breath came in short puffs. "This," he said, waving his hand across the table. "Two cups of coffee. Two sets of shoes side by side in the living room. Two place settings at the table."

Simone's brow wrinkled. "I'm not sure what you're saying."

Gabe's mouth lifted in a smile as he repeated her words. "Try to keep up, Glory. I'm saying I love you. I want to spend the rest of my life loving you, supporting you, and cheering you on. Whether it's school, or hiking through Spain, or whatever other crazy idea you have, I want to be with you."

Tears flowed down Simone's cheeks as she choked out her answer. "I love you, too, Glory."

Three weeks later -

Gabe adjusted his fireproof suit and tightened the strap leading to the oxygen tank. He glanced over at Simone who sent him a thumbs up. He could barely make out her features behind the scratched faceplate of the yellow headgear.

He raised his faceplate and leaned in to shout in her ear. "It isn't the Camino de Santiago."

Simone smiled and shook her head. "Next year."

"But not for our honeymoon, okay?"

She sent him a sly grin. "We'll see."

The announcer's voice boomed through the temporary sound stage outside the US Bancorp Tower in downtown Portland. Spectators gathered from across the state and beyond to cheer on the first responders who took on the 9/11 Memorial Stair Challenge.

Gabe couldn't believe it when Simone told him she would join him.

"I want to be a part of your world," she'd said. "Every part. Even the tough, scary parts."

Gabe glanced over her head at the crowd and found his parents standing next to Simone's. They'd flown in for a day just for this moment. Olivia grinned from her wheelchair, white bandage on her head brilliant in the sun.

The two sets of parents had formed an immediate bond. Hope settled into his spirit. Hope was the missing element in his past relationship with Tiffany. He'd made peace with her and with God and was ready to step into the future with this amazing woman by his side.

He mouthed the words 'I love you.' He watched her lips as she said the same.

"Ready?" Gabe held out his hand as the announcer shouted, "Go!"

Simone took his hand, and they began to climb.

AUTHOR'S NOTE:

Each 9/11 Memorial Stair Climb participant pays tribute to a FDNY firefighter by climbing or walking the equivalent of the 110 stories of the World Trade Center. Your individual tribute not only remembers the sacrifice of an FDNY brother, but symbolically completes their heroic journey to save others. Through firefighter and community participation we ensure that each of the 343 firefighters is honored and that the world knows that we will never forget. These 9/11 Memorial Stair Climbs help the National Fallen Firefighters Foundation create and maintain programs that support fire service survivors. Your support of the 9/11 Memorial Stair Climb events provides assistance to the surviving families and co-workers of the 343 firefighters who made the ultimate sacrifice on September 11, 2001. - https://www.firehero.org/events/9-11-stair-climbs/

Consider getting involved in this remembrance by visiting the above website. Thank you to all the brave firefighters who gave everything to help their fellow men and women.

Follow me on Social Media here:https://linktr.ee/jdalyauthor?utm_source=linktree_admin_share

Other books from Winged Publications:

Hearts of Main Series
Her Forever Home https://amzn.to/45tzllE
The Pastor's Perfect Wife https://amzn.to/3W7WIg9

www.ingramcontent.com/pod-product-compliance
Lightning Source LLC
Chambersburg PA
CBHW070416310726
48977CB00003B/712